THE JEWISH DOG

Asher Kravitz

PENLIGHT PUBLICATIONS

The Jewish Dog
By Asher Kravitz

Translated by Michal Kessler

Edited by Shari Dash Greenspan

English Translation Copyright © 2015 by Penlight Publications/Urim Publications

This is a work of fiction. Names, characters, places, and incidents are either the product of the author's imagination or are used fictitiously, and any resemblance to any actual persons living or dead, events, or locales, is entirely coincidental.

Originally published in Hebrew
as *HaKelev HaYehudi* by Yedioth Ahronoth in 2007

Typeset by Ariel Walden
Cover design by the Virtual Paintbrush

First edition. Printed in Israel.

ISBN: 978-098-386-853-8

Library of Congress Control Number: 2014908073

Penlight Publications
527 Empire Blvd., Brooklyn, New York 11225 USA
Tel: 718-288-8300 Fax: 718-972-6307

www.PenlightPublications.com

For Wawa,
spark of my existence, root of my soul,
salt of my tears, my blood –
for teaching me the meaning of the verse
"Take now thy son, thine only son. . . ."

THE JEWISH DOG

Look at me, brethren, sullen with grief,
   beaten, shamed, and chased by brutes.
A wandering Jew, a driven leaf,
   dodging sticks and kicks and boots.

PROLOGUE

As far back as I can remember, I've walked around completely in the nude. Naked I came from my mother's womb and naked I walked the face of the earth all the years of my life. I am not an exhibitionist. On the contrary, life has taught me that, as a rule, I'm better off staying out of the spotlight. I simply live by other norms. At the risk of seeming ignorant or narrow-minded, I'll admit it – I'm illiterate. I don't understand how reading a book will benefit me in any way. So what do I take interest in? Food! First and foremost, food! Besides that, there's no use denying that I take some interest in the fairer sex, though I can't, to my dismay, boast about any grand conquests. In fact, I've only ever had one serious relationship. She was as beautiful as a summer's day. Lovely and temperate. Her name was Margo, and the fact that she refused, in an act of feminist defiance, to shave her legs, didn't lessen her attractiveness. I often think about our last night together, homeless, in the fierce cold. Even the white-hot rays of love couldn't thaw my body on that cursed night . . . until those men in dark coats came along. I wonder if they managed to drug her too.

In any case, despite the deep feelings I still have for Margo, I won't deny that I look at other females. Casual sex, in my humble opinion, is not to be frowned upon. It's a part of life, just as the abundance of food served every day at home doesn't supersede the joy of grabbing a quick meal off the side of the road. Yes, food. Food, food, and once again – food. Food is, without a doubt, the most important thing in life. It's not hard to understand that there were days that I starved. I went through long months in which every sausage skin was a treasure in my eyes. There were weeks that I lived off potato peels, and each morsel of moldy bread tasted like biscuits and gravy. Sometimes, to fool my hunger, I would chew on pieces of wood or soles of shoes. Nevertheless, my obsession with food shouldn't be ascribed to my days of hunger. Food is paramount – that was seared into my mind from the crystallization of my identity, and that was that.

I was born to and raised by a single mother. At the time, there was minimal awareness of the issue and my family's single-parent status didn't win us any benefits. Due to the circumstances, my dedicated mother was forced to care for us on her own. I'm innocent of any Oedipal complex. I've never had the urge to hurt my father, and it's no wonder – I've never met him. My mother wouldn't mention him, at least not in my presence. From the few rumors and scraps of gossip that I managed to pick up, it seems that my father was a nameless low-life. Judging by my looks, he had brown eyes and large, hairy ears. It's odd that my mother, with all her fancy ancestry, chose him.

Although it's inappropriate for a child to think about the intimate moments of his conception, it's tempting to picture the situation. My mother runs away and finds refuge in the bushes, where her lover awaits her. They don't have time for excessive romance or foreplay, and without delay an innocent sperm is dispatched to fertilize my mother's egg. It was a fleeting amorous moment which sentenced me to an existence and to hair-raising hardships the likes of which you've never heard before. And trust me, when it comes to raising hairs, I'm quite the expert.

Mine was a home birth, a common thing back in the day. Upon turning eight days old, I was not circumcised, and I can't say I regret that. I had at least three brothers and one sister. If I were to meet them by chance tomorrow, I highly doubt I would recognize them. I wonder if any of them are still alive, and if so, what they're up to. None of their names have ever been mentioned in the Search Bureau for Missing Relatives radio broadcasts.

My eldest brother, only a few minutes older than me, had a habit of sneaking up on me, catching me by the legs, and flipping me on my back. He found much amusement in this romp. I was scared of him because he was stronger than me, but I pretended to view it as a game. There was no use trying to run from him – he was much faster. Sometimes I would turn to my mother and ask her to rein him in, but she would watch his abusive actions with a compassionate, motherly gaze, and wouldn't do a thing. Again and again she would explain to me that these games are crucial.

"Life is an endless battle – and you must learn to survive. You'll see," she would say. "When your brother is taken away, you'll miss him very much."

Before she could even finish preaching, my sneaky brother would be storming toward me, prepared to knock me to the floor. If it weren't for the carpet, my whole body would have been covered in bruises, welts, and wounds. I would lie down and look sadly at my mother – perhaps she'd reevaluate her educational approach. How deluded was I! It was clear that she saw her eldest son's behavior as nothing but playful shenanigans, and she had no intention of intervening.

I wouldn't want to be that guy who blames his parents' mistakes for all of his shortcomings, but the truth is that my mother never changed my diaper, never told me a bedtime story, and never put money under my pillow when one of my teeth fell out. What could I expect? After I was born, she ate our placenta. And besides, Mother was only two-and-a-half years older than me.

CHAPTER 1

From the very beginning, I knew I was an exceptional pup. In fact, my opinion on the matter has never changed. There are countless things that distinguish me from my fellow dogs. The first is my understanding that all good things must come to an end – said end usually being much closer than expected. I envy those who linger carelessly at their master's feet, exposing an expectant belly with the utmost trust. I am not among them. Something in me always keeps me on my toes. Even if I do let myself succumb to the occasional petting, I'm always prepared for the calamities lurking right around the corner. My vigilance is incurable. Acknowledging that everything in life is temporary is a cornerstone of my Jewish identity.

My ability to recognize the transient stems from a well-developed awareness of time. Lodged in my mother's womb, the membranes of my mind winding and entwining in an ingenious molecular dance, I became aware that my existence alongside the placenta would soon come to an end. Crammed inside with so many others, there wasn't much room for doubt; our present reality would have to be replaced with another.

The overcrowding was annoying and frustrating, yet the hopeless optimism of youth urged me to see the glass as half full. The many difficult weeks inside the womb had their advantages. The greatest was that I didn't have to spend every waking moment struggling for food. This luxury left me with plenty of time for contemplation. Muffled echoes from the outside world entered the bubble of my being. For the first time I recognized, albeit vaguely, the cyclical nature of the world: a time of hustle and bustle, a time of peace and quiet; a time of frenzy, a time of rest; a time to feed, a time to digest. I mulled over an impossible quandary: was it worth replacing my current existence with another? My heart said nay. I preferred to stay with the devil I knew.

Bit by bit, my siblings and I took our final shapes. The congestion impeded our ability to move around. With stumps for tails and partially formed extremities, each looming life tried to secure for itself the space it needed. When the pressure from the walls of the womb became unbearable, my fetal mind accepted the decree: against my will I shall be born, and against my will I shall live.

And the birth itself? Cliché dictates that it's an amazing experience, and that everyone should be born at least once. Indeed I was born only once. (As to the number of times I've almost died – at some point I stopped counting.) The compulsion for survival is another building block of my Jewish identity. I'd even go so far as to say that my Jewish brethren would do well to take a lesson from me in survival.

Today, looking back with the 20-20 hindsight of twelve

years, I remember my birth as a moment of clarity. Although the birth itself was little more than a jumble of amniotic fluid and chaos, from the very first moment I felt a wonderful lucidity. The voices, a dull echo in the womb, were sharpened tenfold, and they carried with them some of the wealth and plenty that was awaiting me, or so I believed. The wonderful sharpness of sound immediately verified what I had assumed while floating aimlessly: my brothers and I were not alone in the world.

The contact with the carpet, the cold floor below, my brothers tumbling upon me in a maelstrom of body parts, the newfound freedom of movement, the blind attempts to feel my way toward Mother, and the never-ending murmurs of the world – all of these left little room for doubt: being born is an amazing experience, and at its pinnacle – the first experience of sniffing. But it would be some time until I learned to recognize every detail in the wave of scents and odors, the hidden information carried in each waft of air reaching my wet nostrils. An endless concoction of perfumes, disinfectants, animals in heat, tobacco, burning benzene, the oily spreads with which humans polish their shoes, bodily secretions, cut grass, gunpowder, and food. Yes, food. That first scent of food marked the beginning of my passion for nourishment. I made my way head first through the narrow path to my mother's life-giving teats. That was the start of the war of existence.

Indeed, the memories from my suckling days include a lot of pushing and pulling. The food supply was limited, and if you didn't push, you didn't eat. After the battle for food, my siblings and I would make up quickly. We held no grudges. The bitterness was quickly forgotten and we played together good-naturedly. There were no hard feelings.

"Mother, Mother, come!" Reizel called eagerly. "Bruriah gave birth. Six puppies!"

Herschel and Joshua also urged their mother to come see the marvel.

Herschel, Joshua, and Reizel's calls of excitement were the first utterances, the first words I heard in the human tongue. Without attempting to rewrite the past, it was clear to me that my new state – this so-called "life" – was closely tied to the children whose voices I heard then for the very first time. Though my eyes were still closed, I saw this basic truth clearly.

From man's confident voice, I learned that he holds the position of strength. His scent of authority was so absolute that I entertained the possibility that dogs and humans are not the same species at all. The voices emitted by these creatures – who smelled strongly of mastery – contributed to the notion that sprung into my mind ever so early, developing and growing over the years into a well-defined hypothesis: dogs and men are not the same.

I experienced a restless urge to understand the language of man. In those days, I had not yet deciphered the meaning of my mother's barks, but it was easy to find some rhyme and reason in them. However, the muffled grunts of the two-legged seemed incomprehensible. At this point, I could barely understand the children's speech. Listening to them contributed little to my budding vocabulary, as their conversations were boisterous and their diction poor.

But I wouldn't throw up my paws. I was firm in my decision – I would find a way to decipher human speech. My thirst for knowledge even eclipsed my hunger for food.

Only a handful of days passed, and I already acquired my first three words. The first three treasures in my hoard. A heap of words that has multiplied at an impressive rate since those days of yore, if I may say so myself. My first three words were related, and yet I was unable to put my finger on the nuances. The words were "eww," "yuck," and "*gevald.*" All three were said in a reprimanding tone and were associated with the relief of emptying my bladder on the kitchen floor.

"Kitchen" was the magical, mysterious name of the place from which intoxicating scents wafted day and night. Several times a day, I would arise from my mother's resting mat and toddle toward the source of the appetizing odors. The scents emanating from the kitchen, especially when Shoshana's friend Marta came to cook with her, put me in a stupor. With utmost concentration, I would take in the smells of Shoshana's marvelous cuisine.

Even after being rebuked, I would relieve myself on the same spot on the kitchen floor, time and time again. But then, relief was joined by guilt and embarrassment. I felt like a criminal, unwillingly led by his legs once again to the scene of the crime. Later, the word "NO" joined the party. This word was hurled at me over and over, when chewing on what I later learned to be a "rug," or upon resting my paws on the elevated throne of man, which came to be known as a "couch."

Building my vocabulary was, to me, the most pressing

matter. During my first days upon this earth, when I still had little idea of what was actually going on around me, I was careful to listen closely to the speech of man, and file every utterance he made in the recesses of my mind. Many sentences were seared into my memory even though I didn't understand them. Later they would surface, their meanings clarified. Thankfully, I was blessed with a sharp memory – I am a dog who never forgets. This too I attribute to the Jewish blood flowing through my veins. "Thou shalt not forget!"

It is important to note that even when I could only count the words I knew on two paws, I was able to understand the gist of what was being said according to both the intonation and the scent wafting from the speaker's body. I recognized without difficulty whether they were growls of joy, words of love, or snarls of anger and derision.

The first time I heard cries of disgust was when, much to my embarrassment, a tick was found in my fur.

"What is this ugly thing? Eww!" Reizel cried.

"A tick!" Herschel declared.

Joshua, who also wanted to see the despicable creature sucking my blood, called for help. "Daddy! He has a tick on his ear!"

Kalman, the father of the three, touched the tick with the edge of his cigarette, and it shriveled and died instantaneously. That was the first I learned of the health hazards associated with cigarettes.

The ticks were unbearable, but my true nemesis has always been the flea. Every time I think about these low organisms, a shiver runs down my spine. Imagine tiny, despicable creatures crawling across your skin, and you have no way of stopping them. The feeling is ten times worse during your first few weeks of life, when you're still cast in darkness. Until this day, I wake with a start when my puppyhood returns to me in my dreams. The children pinch my skin and taunt "flea, flea. . . ."

The fleas helped me mark an important distinction – the body is divided in two: the places you can reach with your teeth and tongue, and the rest of your body. When the fleas roam the areas beyond the reach of my tongue, I lose my mind.

A more pungent odor than that of disgust is the odor of termination. Through my shut eyelids, I first encountered death. One of my brothers, a nameless pup, didn't have enough strength to make his way to Mother's milk. As we raced to her teats, my siblings and I disregarded any fraternal considerations. The weaker brother was left behind. As he lost strength, his chances of gaining his daily portion diminished. His fate was sealed. Mother stopped feeding and licking him. I realized that the improvement in my own condition was a direct result of my brother's misfortune, but I was amazed at how easy it is to bear the suffering of another when extra milk, extra space at my mother's side, and extra quality time under her tongue are blinding your conscience.

"Mama, look," said Joshua. "I think one of the puppies is sick."

Joshua's father came and lifted my brother. "Yes," he said. "He looks very weak, and his nose is completely dry."

"Oh no," Joshua said. "Look. His head is dropping. . . ."

Kalman did not respond.

That scent was seared into my mind forever. The scent of death.

After the evening feeding, we curled up, exhausted, deep inside my mother's thick fur to sleep. In the still of the night, I had my first dream: huge teats filled with milk just for me, no struggle required. The sounds of the passing day also resurfaced in my mind. It was during sleep that the slurred sounds were formed into an initial understanding.

During the first weeks, I heard Reizel, Joshua, and Herschel's mother, Shoshana, repeat to them, "Don't give them names! If you give them names, you'll become emotionally attached and it'll be ten times harder to give them away."

The matter of giving names contributed to my gut feeling that humans and dogs were separate beings. It was hard for me to understand the deep human compulsion to name every object and creature.

Even Matilda, whom I eventually identified as the housekeeper, was asked not to name us. Despite my temporary blindness, I could tell that Matilda had a different and disorienting scent. The fundamental rule that every living being has a scent, either of "belonging" or "not belonging," didn't apply in her case. She gave off a surprising blend of both.

At this point, the children gave me and my siblings temporary nicknames that weren't considered real, official names. My eldest brother was called "the biggest." I was "the white one with the black circle around his eye and brown patch on his chest." We shared our cushion with "the female," "the cross-eyed one," and "the one with the crooked tail."

Without a proper name or the ability to see, my imagination was somewhat poor. The fact that I received the name "the white one with the black circle around his eye and brown patch on his chest" didn't contribute to my sense of self. Who am I? With no name or image, who can guarantee that I truly exist? Who can guarantee that I am not just a figure in another dog's dream?

In my distress, I did what any other reasonable dog would do – I barked.

I bark, therefore I am.

CHAPTER 2

*A*nd then I opened my eyes.

The first thing I saw was my mother. Things were coming together: the teats of milk, the sniffing snout, and the moist tongue. Everything was set in place, exactly as I had pictured it. But it wasn't just that; I couldn't look away. I stared at her, mesmerized. Mother was beautiful. Her looks made a deep impression on me: a magnificent tail, speckled fur, broad shoulders, and paws large and stable.

The rest of the world – which at this point amounted to the living room of the Gottlieb house – also suddenly took shape. From east to west, from north to south, and up and down – all was ruled by the Gottliebs. At the time, the Gottliebs seemed to me – an innocent puppy who barely reached their ankles – like giants, able to stand on their hind legs by the grace of some divine power. Their ability to stand for such a long time without leaning on their front legs reinforced my hypothesis that dogs and men were inherently different, and did not only differ in the density of their fur.

In retrospect, I believe the Gottliebs also knew very early on that I was different from my siblings. Our playing habits revealed that immediately. My brothers would play to the point of exhaustion. I would act in a more thoughtful and reserved manner. At the end of play time, my siblings would collapse, exhausted, and while away their days sleeping. I wasn't like that. I preferred pondering to playing. My brothers played like there was no tomorrow, suckled beyond their capacity, and slept endlessly. I played only to appease my mother. Mostly, I would sit in a corner and muse.

The subject of my brooding was usually the human being. Listening to their speech and watching their actions gave me new insights every day. I scrutinized every movement made by a Gottlieb and examined their body language: a nod of the head, a wrinkling of the eyebrows, every flutter, subtle as it may be.

The Gottlieb children enjoyed lifting me up and shaking me in front of their faces, squishing me affectionately, and murmuring sweet nothings. Frankly, I didn't enjoy being lifted, and it usually made me need to pee. However, being held with my nose just an inch from the children's gave me a great opportunity to observe their faces from licking distance. Their sparse fur was distributed illogically, most of it placed at the top of their heads. How odd these creatures were. Their noses were but a tiny pyramid, barely protruding, and their mouths just a horizontal slit, dividing their flat elliptical faces. Inside their mouths was a short tongue, much shorter than my mother's, and their teeth were laughably dull. Bit by bit, these observations bore fruit. I was astonished to discover that humans wouldn't hang their tongues out, even if they were very hot. I learned that the Gottliebs were able to use their front paws to pick fleas and ticks, open the pantry, place records on the gramophone, and attach a leash to a collar.

I didn't only learn about the skills humans possessed, but about their limitations as well. When there was a knock on the door, Shoshana would tell her children: "Go see who it is and what they want!" Were they unable to smell the identity of the man standing outside? Is it possible that their tiny noses were so useless?

There was one instance that proved to me, once and for all, that the human sense of smell was very limited indeed. Herschel and Joshua were in a mischievous mood and asked Reizel if she felt like eating a piece of apple strudel. Reizel responded enthusiastically, and was quick to sink her teeth into the pastry they handed her. Two bites were enough. Revolted, she spit out what she had already chewed. "You're disgusting!" she shouted, chasing her brothers into the courtyard. "Disgusting! Disgusting! Disgusting! I hate you and I hate potato knish!"

"You're so gullible!" The brothers burst out laughing at their sister's frustration, while I stayed in the kitchen wondering how she could have made such a mistake and devoured the remains of the counterfeit pastry.

Word by word and phrase by phrase, my vocabulary grew. I learned that "leash" and "key" were often said before taking me out. Putting on a coat, tying shoelaces, turning the key, and picking up the leash were clear indicators of a walk.

The walks took place in the realm called "outside," which is the opposite of "inside." There was a huge wall separating the two, and they were as different from one another as hot and cold. Inside, urinating was strictly forbidden. Outside, it was not only allowed, it was commended. Each time I emptied my bladder outside, I was showered with words of encouragement and praise. I couldn't understand how Kalman could be so impressed and excited about an outdoor urination when he completed impossible feats every day.

One such miraculous feat was lighting cigarettes. Kalman masterfully controlled the smoke rings coming out of his mouth. To myself, I called Kalman "woooof woof woof woof woooof," meaning "master of fire." Another interesting observation I made about the difference between me and my brothers and the humans was our social habits: we would play all day, and as the sun came down, we'd huddle together for a warm and cuddly night's sleep. The humans did the exact opposite. During the day, the family would often sit together, but at night, Kalman and his wife would go into an alcove meant exclusively for them, and the children went each to his or her own separate cranny.

In order to enter the living chambers, a complex action of turning a doorknob was required. Such an action was far beyond the scope of my motor skills. At a very young age I developed feelings of hostility toward doors. Windows, however, were a different story. I was a huge fan. I especially liked the window in the guest room, which had a fantastic view of the street. I discovered it just a few days after opening my eyes, and since then, not a day went by that I didn't watch the hustle and bustle of the world right below my snout for a couple of hours at least. The peacefulness of the hours I spent observing was disturbed only by the angry barks coming from the opposite side of the street. In a window of a grey brick building across the way, there was a large dog. He'd bark at me often, his jaws open wide. His head was massive and black, and his droopy ears would bounce as a warning signal with every bark. Sometimes my mother would hurry to the window and respond with her own salvo of barks.

I believe that, for a canine, I was blessed with extraordinary sight. Though my world was mostly comprised of sounds and smells, I was also able to enjoy the visual. I was especially fascinated with the creatures traveling the roads at amazing speeds, clattering by. They never had to stop to relieve themselves.

"Why doesn't the white one with the black circle around his eye and brown patch on his chest ever stop barking at the automobiles?" Reizel asked her mother.

"I have no idea," Shoshana responded. "Ask your father."

"Father, why doesn't the white one with the black circle around his eye and brown patch on his chest ever stop barking at the automobiles?"

"Maybe he has strong sheepdog instincts," Kalman observed. "Maybe he thinks they're cows, trying to escape the herd."

Though yours truly couldn't understand a fraction of Kalman's learned answer, I could sense with some satisfaction that the Gottliebs were as curious about me as I was about them. At the end of the day, whether my barks could be scientifically explained or not, I stuck to my habit of barking at the cars, and I wouldn't withhold barks from

horses either, as they trotted below the window. Not one of
them heeded my barks.

I spent most of my spare time with my siblings and mother
on the living room carpet. As I mentioned already, I was
endowed with exceptional curiosity, and the décor in the
room caught my attention. The bureau in the corner of
the living room held pictures of the Gottliebs' ancestors.
Shoshana liked to point them out to every new acquain-
tance that paid a visit. "Rabbi Meir Israel Lieb Gottlieb,
Kalman's father," she would say, pointing at the thick frame.
Rabbi Meir Israel Lieb Gottlieb's likeness had an owl-like
gaze, a white beard, and ears like a pampered poodle. I
think I recognized a certain resemblance between the face
in the frame and Kalman. "And this is his wife, Bubbe Sarah
Leah, may she rest in peace." Grandma Sarah Leah's eyes
were as sad as a pup with a biscuit held just out of reach.

Of course, at that point I was unable to conjure up a
family tree in my mind. Not of my adoptive family nor of
my biological family. The Gottliebs were often asked by
neighbors about my mother's breed. "She's a Caucasian
shepherd," the Gottliebs responded, not without a hint
of pride. "Her pedigree is documented seven generations
back."

I understood my neighbors' curiosity. There was no
dog quite as spotted and spectacular as my mother. Her
fur was thick and strewn with patches of black, grey, and
white. Her paws bore matching white socks, her teeth
were white and unblemished, and her coiled tail was

adorned with long, soft fur. I could do nothing but watch and admire.

Despite my mother's beauty and pedigree, I quickly understood that her place in the broader hierarchy – four-legged and two-legged combined – was not as high as I had first surmised. My esteem for my mother diminished when I understood that the Gottliebs, and the Gottliebs alone, controlled the light. There were chandeliers hanging from the ceiling, upside-down shrubs with flowers that produced light. The family members determined when there would be light in the room by using a small switch by the door. The Gottliebs could make light into darkness and darkness into light – ordinances of heaven and earth! But the light and the dark are but an example. In fact, one could say that humans controlled everything.

And my mother? I woefully learned that her only responsibilities were nursing, carrying my brothers and me by our napes, and naturally, bathing us with her tongue whenever she was so inclined. Humans, on the other hand, determined everything. They determined when we'd go out for a walk, when meals would be served, and how much food would be set in our bowls. Of all their magical powers, I was most jealous of their ability to open and close doors. If only I could change the state of a door so easily: open, closed, open.

Naming was also the authority of the Gottliebs, and whatsoever they called every living creature, that was its name thereafter. When my mother was adopted, they named her Bruriah. They selected her name as a sign of honor for her wisdom and splendor. They were very impressed with her ability to sit, lie down, bark, reach out her right paw, reach out her left paw, and roll over on demand. Every time she displayed her skills, she was rewarded with a piece of chicken or a rich beef bone. I made up my mind to acquire the same skills, forthwith.

CHAPTER 3

*O*nce we were weaned off Mother's milk, Reizel, Joshua, and Herschel's friends began visiting our home, accompanied by their parents. The young visitors would try to convince their parents to adopt one of the puppies. Fritz Leiter, Joshua's friend, was torn between me and my oldest brother. I wanted to impress him, but my tail jerked suddenly in a strange and involuntary motion. I tried to catch it in my mouth, but no matter how fast I turned, my tail was always one step ahead. Eventually, I surrendered to my dizziness and fell on my back. Fritz told Joshua that he was not interested in a stupid dog, and took my brother home. Several hours later, I parted with my sister, who was taken by a young girl named Helena Luntz.

And then there were three.

"Daddy," asked Reizel, "don't you think Bruriah is sad that we're giving away her puppies?"

"We'll only give her puppies to good families," Kalman promised.

More young boys came with their parents. The conversations were almost identical.

"What a beautiful dog! Let's adopt him!"

"And who will feed him? And who will take him out on walks?"

"We will."

"And when the excitement dies down, who will take your dog out for walks?"

"We will take care of him forever."

"And what will happen when you get drafted into the army?"

That question remained unanswered.

"'We will take care of him forever . . .'" Kalman imitated the conversations as soon as the empty-handed speakers departed. "'And what will happen when you get drafted into the army?' Not that the parents intended, God forbid, to ask what would happen to their children's pure souls when they'd shell hospitals and crush innocents under their tanks. They just wanted to know whether the burden of walking the dog would fall on their shoulders."

"You're exaggerating," Shoshana told him. "Hitler talks a lot, but talking about war is not the same as waging war."

"Do you really think I'm exaggerating? And what about the passports that I need to arrange?"

"Bureaucracy at the Ministry of Interior is a pain in the neck, but it's not quite war. By the way, have you taken care of that yet? If you want, I can go. I'll be near City Hall tomorrow anyway."

Before Kalman could respond, Joshua barged into the kitchen, bursting with an idea. "We're three children," he said, "and we now have three puppies. So if we leave the puppies at home, each of us will have our own puppy."

"That's some very impressive numerical symmetry," Kalman responded. "But we decided we have to give the puppies away."

"If not all of them, can't we have at least two?"

Kalman shook his head and Shoshana said, "No!"

"If only we could just keep one puppy. . . ."

"No! Only Bruriah stays! We must give away the puppies!"

Shoshana clarified: "Bruriah is exceptionally bright, but her puppies don't seem to be that smart. Bruriah is purebred and noble, but her mongrel puppies don't look like anything special. Bruriah is very careful about the rules of hygiene, but her puppies, God have mercy, can't tell the living room from the lavatory."

Weeks went by and a new home for us was still not found. As the number of visits from young friends dwindled, Matilda became the next natural candidate. Shoshana and Kalman asked her if she'd be interested in adopting one of us.

"I would love to take one of them, I really would," Matilda said. "Unfortunately, I can't. You don't know my husband. He would never allow an untrained pup to come and soil our house. On the other hand," Matilda began, the spark of a new idea in her eyes. "Remember Uncle Siegfried, whom I told you about? The one whose wife fell ill over the summer?"

Shoshana nodded.

"His dogs are very old. He recently mentioned that he'd like a new dog or two. He needs good dogs to help guard his sheep enclosure." Matilda promised she would talk to her uncle about taking two of us.

"And it's possible," she said, "that Uncle Siegfried will be able to come by to visit as early as next week."

And thus, the question remained: which of the three of us would stay? Reizel declared that she could not choose. Joshua was fond of "the one with the crooked tail." Herschel of "the one with the black circle around his eye and the brown patch on his chest." Meaning, me. Generally speaking, you could say that I was Herschel's favorite, and Herschel was mine. He was the only one of the three siblings who dared disobey his parents and sneak me food during mealtimes. I was astute enough to understand that the food I was receiving was strictly under the table, and I was careful to eat it discreetly. Herschel also let me sneak into his room in the dead of night to share his bed, and he would never turn his face away when I thanked him with a grateful lick on the cheek.

Herschel would relentlessly try to convince his siblings. "Look how cute the white one with the black circle around his eye and brown patch on his chest is." Seeing the look of sublime happiness on the faces of the children each time I did something that was considered "adorable," I came to understand that I had to do as many "adorable" things as possible in order to stay with the family. I pretended that there was no pup as eager as I was to satisfy his owners. All it took was a peek from a member of the family and I started wagging my tail. I stopped pulling randomly on my leash, and each time one of the children came near me, I'd curl up at their feet, reducing myself to a soft and warm little ball of fur. I discovered my manipulative side. "Aww, he's so adorable," Shoshana melted when I went to sleep with my front paws in Kalman's slippers.

With tremendous effort, I taught myself to stand on my back legs for five seconds straight, while pawing the air with my front legs. When Herschel threw sandwich pieces, I caught them in my mouth in midair. The children emitted cries of jubilation. I would hold a paw out to family members and rest my head on their knees. I was always rewarded with soft petting and looks of compassion, confirming my theory that all my brown-nosing and dog tricks would indeed achieve the ultimate goal.

Thus it transpired that my two brothers were given to Matilda's Bavarian uncle, and I was left, for the time being, in the safety of my mother's bosom on the Gottliebs' living room carpet.

"Mother," begged Reizel, Joshua, and Herschel. "Maybe we can just keep the last one?"

She didn't even bother responding directly. "You know the answer. When we find a home for him, he will be given away."

CHAPTER 4

The decree was made following a unique and unforgettable evening that the family called "Seder Night." He who has not seen Seder Night in the Gottlieb household has not witnessed true happiness. From my present sagacious perspective at my advanced age of twelve years, and from my deep familiarity with the Jewish calendar, I can unequivocally say that Passover, the holiday of freedom, is undoubtedly the most important holiday. *Sukkos* is very nice, and I did indeed enjoy sleeping outside in the dog-*sukkah* built for me by Herschel and Joshua as an add-on to the family *sukkah*. And the Hanukkah *latkes* and Purim *hamantaschen* were delicious, don't get me wrong, but Passover is, beyond all shadow of a doubt, the genuine article.

That fateful Seder night, the Gottliebs had invited their friends Marta and Hirsch Jacobson and their children. Marta spent the entire morning with Shoshana in the kitchen, where they diligently prepared the holiday delicacies. Tormented by the intoxicating fragrances, I thought evening would never arrive. Marta spent hours making *charoses* and *eingemachtes*. A wonderful fragrance of black radish, burnt sugar, and almonds filled the kitchen. Shoshana fried eggs for *ayer-lokshen*. She soaked *matzos* in chicken soup, and added bone marrow to make *kneidlach*. She tasted a bit from the ladle and sprinkled another pinch of salt! What torturous aromas! I felt as though the tip of my snout was about to be torn off my face. Toward the afternoon, they worked together to make *kartofelnik*. Shoshana grated potatoes and Marta scrambled eggs, crumbled *matzos*, and mixed it all with savory chicken fat. For an hour and a half, the house was filled with fragrances that kept me from focusing on anything but the marvelous dishes in the oven. Then it was time. The *kartofelnik* was taken out of the oven, baked and browned. Marta tapped on her masterpiece lightly with a spoon, and the hollow sound that resonated from the dish confirmed that it was ready. That was it. I could take it no more. I felt as though I had died; the tempting aroma wafting from that potato casserole had long pushed me past my pain threshold.

Herschel, Reizel, and Joshua wanted to pinch a bit of *charoses* and nibble on the crunchy edges of the *kartofelnik*, but Shoshana forbade them from eating before dinner, and sentenced them all to naps so they wouldn't be conquered by weariness before it was time to sing *Chad Gadia*. I, too, although not expressly asked, curled up in a living room corner and dozed off.

Much to my chagrin, the night started off on the wrong paw. For the first part of the Seder (up until *yachatz*) I was locked up in Shoshana and Kalman's bedroom. The reason: one of the guests, Moishe Jacobson, would howl and yowl each time I came close. When the scent of his fear reached my nostrils, my chest swelled with pride. For the first time in my life, I felt powerful, masculine, and intimidating. The pride was then banished by scorn – how is he not ashamed to be afraid of an adorable little creature like me? Finally, the scorn was replaced by a sudden gust of aggression. I felt an overpowering urge to bite something. I pounced with all the might my four tiny legs could muster, and caught the hem of Herschel's pants in my jaws. Herschel shook his leg to and fro, trying to shake me off, but I just tightened my grip and refused to relent. It was an exciting game. Herschel, who enjoyed seeing my playful spirit, took my head between his hands and growled encouragingly. Alas, the game that caused so much joy for me and Herschel filled Moishe's heart with fear, and I soon found myself behind a locked door. The tantalizing scents of hard-boiled eggs, *gefilte* fish, and well-done roast beef reached my snout by way of the small crack between the door and the floor. I barked my frustration, but Kalman commanded me to be quiet. I had no choice but to lie silently on the floor and let out the occasional whimper.

My mother approached the door from the outside. It saddened her to hear my whimpering, but she wasn't locked up with me because Moishe wasn't scared of her. My mother was serene and mature. She would spend most of her time in the corner, not engaging in juvenile antics like me. Suddenly the door opened. The great burst of light that pervaded the room blinded me. From darkness to great light. Herschel was standing in the doorway. He kneeled by my side and whispered in my ear, "Joshua and I asked Moishe to give you another chance. Behave yourself!"

"You see, Moishe?" Herschel explained as he stroked my forehead. "This puppy is called 'the white one with the black circle around his eye and brown patch on his chest.' There's nothing to be afraid of, he's a small and harmless puppy."

"Come, Moishe," the little coward's mother called. "Pet him." After being promised a spoonful of *charoses*, he agreed to pet me, with certain stipulations. He would pet my back and nothing else, and on the strict condition that my head and canine teeth would be kept far away from him.

When the terms were set and Moishe's reward guaranteed, I received my petting. His pet was little more than a fleeting graze from a terrified, trembling hand. After a few of these finger-tipped attempts, he placed his small palm on my back and ran it through my fur in a real petting. He broke into a proud smile, one befitting a heroic warrior safely returning from the battlefield.

Once the ice was broken, we could move on with the ceremony. Twenty diners, their seats cushioned by pillows, reading from their books, offering their own interpretations, telling stories, and asking questions. I must interpose that, even without understanding the content of the questions (my vocabulary not yet being up to snuff), I got the feeling that they already knew all the answers.

Kalman asked his children to read from the book, insisting on the precise pronunciation of every Hebrew word. After the children tried their hands at reading, Kalman summarized the plot for them. "The Egyptians, led by Pharaoh, plotted to wipe out the Jews. For many years, they ruthlessly enslaved the Jews until God took pity. God plagued the Egyptians, sending frogs, lice, wild animals, and hail to make their lives miserable. They were suitably punished for their sins, and throughout the streets of Egypt, not a dog barked on the night of their clandestine escape."

"And now," Shoshana turned to the young participants. "Now you must find the *Afikomen!*"

The children scattered throughout the house, opening and closing doors, moving pictures hanging on the wall, opening closets, and peeking under the couches. Fifteen minutes of searching went by, and the *Afikomen* was still nowhere to be found. I ran among the children, not wanting to feel left out of the commotion, but I had no idea what I was looking for. Herschel, who saw that I was itching to be part of the fun, decided to take advantage of my honed sniffing skills. He held a piece of *matzo* in front of my snout. Now I was in the game. I sniffed the *matzo*, pointed my snout, and lifted one front paw like an experienced hunting hound.

"Onward," Herschel commanded. "Find the *Afikomen!*"

In less than a minute, I was in front of the bureau, pawing at the second drawer, and letting out a series of barks. Disbelieving, the children opened the drawer and smothered me with words of praise, celebrating with the *Afikomen* in their hands. The knowledge that everyone was talking about me, and in a most positive light, gave me great pleasure.

Herschel insisted that I, and I alone, would receive the traditional gift for finding the *Afikomen*.

"What gift does he want?" Shoshana asked.

Herschel put his ear near my snout and pretended that I was whispering a secret.

"He says he wants to stay in our home!"

"No!" Shoshana answered. "Absolutely not! I already told you a hundred times – we are giving away the puppies."

"In that case," Herschel said defiantly, "the white dog with the black circle around his eye and brown patch on his chest will keep the *Afikomen*."

He brought the *matzo* close to my mouth. I stuck my tongue out to taste it, and Herschel quickly pulled it away, a split second before I slobbered all over it.

Shoshana gave her husband a worried look. "Kalman, tell him to cut out the nonsense."

"But Mrs. Gottlieb," Moishe suddenly came through to my defense, "it's not fair. He's a good dog."

"Passover is Passover, and tradition is tradition, Shoshana dear," Kalman said in his convincing voice. "I'm afraid justice is with Herschel and the white dog with the black circle around his eye and brown patch on his chest. Even Moishe agrees with them. . . ."

"Tomorrow the puppy can have some pot roast," Shoshana tried to propose a compromise.

"He stays!" Herschel rejected the proposal.

"All right, we'll see . . ." she extended her hand to get the *Afikomen* from Herschel, but Herschel quickly hid it behind his back. He demanded explicit consent.

"Fine, fine," his mother gave in. "Fine, he can stay. The white one with the black circle around his eye and brown patch on his chest can stay."

Everyone began nibbling on the *Afikomen*, and the hero of the evening was not forgotten. I, too, was given a piece of the magical *matzo*. As soon as I tasted it, I spat out the sliver of tasteless cardboard and turned my head.

"Look at him," Kalman said, pointing at me. "He must

be thinking to himself, 'Is it possible that this fuss was all over a piece of dry and flavorless dough?'"

"He doesn't understand how I can be so bad at bargaining," Shoshana said jokingly.

After the meal, everyone joyously sang the holiday songs. Back then, being but a small and ignorant pup, I didn't understand a word of Aramaic. I couldn't appreciate the existential truth that was folded into the lines, "*Ve'ata calba venashach leshunra . . . ve'ata hutra vehika lechalba* – and then came the dog that bit the cat . . . and then came the stick that hit the dog." Always know who fears you, and whom you must fear.

As I was declared a part of the family, there was a unanimous decision to give me the leftover pot roast. Moishe was given the task of placing the pot roast in my bowl, and he did it gladly. After he set the leftovers down, he looked, satisfied, upon the delight he caused me, and a feeling of righteousness warmed his little heart. It's hard for me to precisely describe the wave of emotions that overtook me at that moment. A bowlful of pot roast! All mine and only mine! I scared myself by growling at Mother when she dared to come close and examine my windfall. That pot roast would come to me in my dreams and would appear before my eyes in the years of famine that were waiting right around the corner.

CHAPTER 5

*T*he morning after Seder Night, Kalman and Reizel took me out for an early walk. Two blocks from our home, I saw a lone dog crossing the street in faltering strides. The dog was thin and his hip bones protruded. His eyes were big and bulging, his fur was patchy, and he was covered in filth. A burst of anger left my chest in a series of loud barks.

"Why is he barking so?" Reizel asked her father, who hurried to shush me and tightened his grip on my collar. I stood on my hind legs, barking incessantly. Something in the pitiable sight of the dog on the other side of the road sparked uncontrollable anger within me. If only Kalman would let go of my leash, I would pounce on the wretched creature, teeth bared.

"It's a stray," Kalman explained to her. "I don't know why, but since the dawn of time there has been an unwritten rule that house dogs don't like strays."

The stray fearfully tucked his tail between his legs and ran to the street corner. Only after he left my field of vision did I relax. It was the first time in my life that I had smelled such a sharp scent of fear on one of my canine brethren.

When we returned from our walk, the Gottlieb family was already convened in the living room.

"Come, sit down," Shoshana said. "It's time to choose a name for him."

Reizel spoke up immediately. "Let's call him Caleb."

"Why should we call him Caleb?" the brothers protested. Kalman and the boys wanted to give me an appropriate, creative name. Shoshana sat silently and watched her family as they searched high and low for the perfect match. Like a stubborn shoe, the names simply didn't fit. For each name, there were countless reasons why not: too heroic, too self-flattering, too long; he isn't brown, he isn't a poodle; too Jewish, too corny.

When the deluge of ideas ceased, there was a contemplative silence in the room, and Shoshana spoke up. "Come to think of it, what's wrong with Reizel's idea? Why don't we call him Caleb?"

Reizel came up to me and sat by my side. I looked at her with a cocked gaze, waiting for the verdict. She pressed a finger to my forehead. "Caleb," she said. "You are Caleb."

I looked at her, puzzled. What exactly was she trying to say?

"I am Reizel," she pointed at herself. "And you," she once again pressed her finger to my forehead, "are Caleb. Do you understand? You are Caleb."

I still wasn't sure.

"I'm Reizel," she pointed again. "And you are Caleb. Caleb is you. You are Caleb."

I barked twice, as a sign of confirmation: "All right, I got it. I am Caleb!"

Reizel hugged me tightly and smiled, showing off a gleaming set of white teeth.

Several days later, I was given a new collar with an identifying tag. I was a real dog now. My new name was ceremoniously displayed in curly letters: $\mathcal{CALEB}$.

The collar had but brushed my neck when the sky darkened. Thick clouds covered the heavens and lightning bolts struck. I approached the open window and looked out. A voice spoke from heaven: **"Thy name shall not be called any more 'the white one with the black circle around his eye and brown patch on his chest' but rather Caleb shall be your name."**

"Yes," I barked. "I know. Reizel already explained the whole thing."

I looked back and saw the children playing obliviously. I knew the voice was addressing only me. I looked again at the clouds, but they quickly dispersed and left behind them a clear blue sky. Below me, the road I was so accustomed to watching stretched out as usual, but everything suddenly seemed to make sense. I felt like I had bitten into the fruit of the tree of knowledge.

The following days were blessedly routine. Every day, my mother and I were taken out for morning and evening walks. Kalman would lead us on a leash. My mother would relieve herself on the large lawn across the road. I preferred emptying my bladder in a series of strategic locations: the lamppost adjacent to the front gate, the fire hydrant at the street corner, and the roots of the apple tree, which accepted the stream of urine with dignity. The public telephone booth next to the newspaper stand proved to be a urination spot that was not to be missed.

The newspaper vendors would call out, announcing this and that to the passersby. Their cries were mostly about a fellow named Hitler. My vocabulary thus far helped me glean from what they said that Hitler, much like myself, was very occupied with the matter of territory. Every time Kalman passed the newspaper stands, I could feel gloom spread through his heart. If Kalman had a tail, it would no doubt be tucked between his legs.

In the afternoons, Kalman would leave Mother at home and take me out for my own walk. I was granted this extra walk, since I had not yet acquired the ability to control my bladder for long periods of time. These afternoon walks were also an opportune time for meeting up with friends. I would regularly meet Karl Gustav. Karl Gustav was the dog who barked at me from his window in the grey building. He was a powerful Rottweiler, and his owner was an old, hunchbacked man. The first time I met Karl Gustav, I feared it would end in a fight, but to my relief, Karl Gustav was surprisingly friendly. He approached me and stood in a position that said "sniff me and I'll sniff you." First he examined me closely, wondering if there was a spark of spunk in me that would endanger his status in the neighborhood. When he was convinced that I was simply looking to play, his face brightened and he barked at me using the informal "you."

When Karl Gustav's stooped owner and Kalman met,

they would turn toward the Rosenpark and let us off our leashes and let us become engrossed in playful running. Our favorite game was a basic version of what is usually called "tag." The rules were simple. Each time, one of us (usually me) took initiative, straightened his front legs on the grass, and lifted his bum and tail skyward – a position that meant: I will run, catch me if you can. First I ran from him, and then he ran from me. You might think that such a game is boring, a game with no end. But we didn't think so. We played with great enthusiasm until our lungs gave out, and we lay on the grass struck by exhaustion, huffing and puffing with our tongues protruding. I barely recognized myself as I played with endless vigor. Was this the same puppy who, in his youth, preferred pondering on the sidelines over playing with his brothers? I hypothesized that home created a relaxing atmosphere, unbefitting any frolicking, whereas the cool breeze and green meadows encouraged more playfulness.

On a handful of occasions, more dogs joined the game. They were all members of the "tag club." The rules of multiple player tag were more complex than the basic tag I played with Karl Gustav – at times the rules would change mid-game. When there was a great number of dogs and the innocent game evolved into a scene of pure chaos, I could feel myself change as well. The pack awakened ancient echoes inside me. The blood of my lupine ancestors began pulsing in my veins. But my wolfishness was lacking. I couldn't connect with my inner wolf the way my fellow "tag club" members could as they ran amok on the grass, biting at one another. My perspective of the world and of myself was already affected by broader understanding and insight. This feeling had intensified since I heard the heavenly voice speak to me. I simultaneously embodied a wild beast and an intelligent dog watching his wolfish brothers with their primitive traditions.

Every now and then, we were joined by Heidi and Brigitte, two pedigree poodles with twenty-thousand mark haircuts. Mostly, they came for a short backside sniff, and waived the invitation to join the game. They watched from a snobbish distance, as though they couldn't care less, and went on their way with their moist snouts raised proudly in the air.

On some walks I met Spitz. A miniature pinscher with a temper, he liked to bark at every passing dog. Spitz was the size of a rodent, and his narrow leash tied him to a young girl who would pull him back and constantly scold him. When the collar around his pinscher neck tightened, he would fall silent for a short moment, and look sourly at the girl, at me, and back at the girl. He would give me a glowering stare and bark at me for no good reason. Spitz's courage lasted mere seconds. When I'd bark back, he would drop his tail and let out a whimper of surrender.

"He's a fraud," Kalman whispered to me with a wink. "A sheep in wolf's clothing." I pointed my ears in agreement and, being unable to wink back, I added a canine nod of the head.

When I would return from my afternoon walks, Mother would hurry to my side and press her nose to mine. I would stand at attention, letting her sniff and examine me closely. I waited patiently until she finished sniffing out every piece of information she could find about the places I had visited and the friends I had met. After Mother was satisfied,

I made my way to my feeding dish and water bowl. The long walk and dynamic game had left me with quite an appetite, and I wolfed down my food quickly, leaving the dish spotless. The family made sure I ate nothing but the food placed in my dish. I was absolutely forbidden to eat out. When I'd try to enrich my diet with food that came my way, I was slapped and scolded. A piece of strudel run over by a truck was still a viable snack in my eyes, but even that was forbidden. Needless to say, cat and horse feces were completely out of the question.

In their defense, the Gottliebs practiced what they preached. They set quite the example for not eating out of the house. Although the reason they avoided restaurants was a matter of *kashrus* while I was forbidden to eat on the street because of hygiene, the fine example they set was a moral stamp of approval to their demands.

There was one café, Tsuzamen, which Kalman would visit from time to time. It was a small neighborhood place that served inexpensive coffee and simple pastries. Because the menu only included dairy products, Kalman allowed himself to have a cup of coffee there as he perused the morning papers. When he went, he would tie me up outside. At first, I didn't make much of it. On the contrary, I was too impressed by his seasoned bartering skills. I watched him through the glass door, handing the owner mere pieces of paper and in return being served coffee and a pastry by the fool. However, as time passed, being tied up became nothing less than an insult. Kalman sat there enjoying his morning coffee while I sat outside, tied to a pole. Even a creature with as few demands as I couldn't pretend that there was nothing wrong with the picture. I named my post "the pillory." I think Kalman was aware of my distress. Every time he tied me up, he would crouch to my level, pet my forehead, and whisper, "don't worry little friend, I won't be long."

The price of abandonment outside the café was well worth the prize of weekends. Every week, I was reminded of the great advantage of belonging to a Jewish pack. Though during the week my food dish usually contained simple leftovers, Friday night brought with it remnants of juicy chicken, strips of beef fat, and fish brine that surpassed the very nectar of the gods. This was the gravy in which the *gefilte* fish swam. If only you could see me wolfing down that wonderful sauce. I consumed the entire dish before you could say "woof."

The fact that I could regularly enjoy such fancy meals added a weekly dimension to my sense of time. The daily dimension was clear and natural; it was directly related to sunrises and sunsets, light and dark, hot and cold, and shadows getting longer and shorter. The monthly cycle had its own physical aspect, tied to the magical power of the moon. The weekly cycle, however, was harder to figure out. Its only indicator was the Shabbos meal. Shabbos meals were very carefully planned events. The Gottliebs would wear their best clothes and stand together around the table. Kalman would lift a glass and sing in his clear voice, "For You have chosen us and sanctified us, of all nations." My mother and I were the only ones in the room allowed to stay seated as he sang. Before the meal began, the family would rise to wash their hands, and would not speak until they broke bread. When I dared to bark between washing and eating, the entire family would look at me with reprimanding looks and silently shush me. It was a family joke that would make everyone smile anew.

During dinnertime, while my mother and I were gobbling down our food, the Gottliebs would supplement their meal with songs and *divrei torah* – short explanations of the weekly Torah portion.

When the meal ended, Shoshana would place strawberries, apples, and pastries on the living room table. Herschel and Joshua would drape a sheet over two chairs and sit together under the makeshift tent. They would employ me as their watchdog, guarding the tent opening. Sometimes Reizel, Herschel, and Joshua would pretend to be puppies. They would join me and my mother on the ground and traverse the carpet on all fours, presenting their heads to Shoshana and Kalman for petting.

There was one trick that Reizel especially liked. She would place a mirror in front of my face and watch my perplexed expression. Who was that Caleb imitating my every movement, watching me with the same puzzled face? The mirrored Caleb had his own Reizel watching him with a satisfied look on her face. The first time Reizel performed the mirror trick, I was struck by confusion. As time went by, I realized that the other Caleb was no more than a copycat lacking any initiative, and I lost interest.

CHAPTER 6

*T*he crisis came on suddenly.

That day was filled with the hustle-bustle of family activity. There was an air of celebration. The living room table was covered with colorfully wrapped gifts, as well as cakes and other delicacies that I was strictly forbidden to touch. Reizel unwrapped a large present, and inside she found a doll wearing a long, frilly dress. "Father, this is from you, right?" Kalman hugged her tightly and said, "My favorite author, Agatha Christie, was also born on September 15th."

"I've read Agatha Christie," Joshua said. Herschel threw him a nasty look that meant "Shut up, you're such a brown noser." Later, Joshua and Herschel sang "Happy Birthday" to their little sister, and Shoshana cut the pear cake. The sense of idyll ended when Kalman turned on the radio.

"It's that Hitler again. You can't switch on the radio without hearing him." Then he added under his breath, "*Der hund bellt!* The dog is barking again!"

Shoshana frowned and said sadly, "Haman was a *Lamed Vovnik** compared to this guy."

I could smell that Kalman's soul was in a rage. I saw that he was getting restless, and when he was restless, he would take me on walks. The knowledge that I would soon go on a walk had me on my toes. Kalman sat for several more minutes with his family before he said, "I can see that Caleb is impatient. I think I should take him out for a little while."

As we passed the park, I saw my friend waiting for me, tail wagging. Kalman let me off my leash and I ran off to play with Karl Gustav. We ran together on the wide grassy hill and played our endless game of tag. We were soon joined by our friends Bomba, Zuga, and Schwart, and our quiet game quickly became a jumble of barking and play-pouncing. I could see Karl Gustav's owner sitting next to Kalman. He leaned over and whispered something into Kalman's ear. Then he pointed to a nearby signpost. Kalman's face clouded over and his mood darkened. I felt as though a black cat had passed between Kalman and his German neighbor. Just then, a black cat passed between me and Karl Gustav too, but to our great joy, this one was not a metaphorical black cat. With newfound exuberance, Karl Gustav began chasing it fervently, and our playmates joined him in a carefully coordinated hunt. I joined the adventure as well. The cat hastily ran and hid in the tall branches of a nearby cherry tree.

By way of habit, I glanced briefly at the bench to make sure that Kalman was still around. Rule of thumb: always make sure that your owner is within sniffing range. I saw

---

* righteous person

Kalman reading the sign with a worried look on his face. But the mere sight of him reassured me, and I could dedicate my full attention to the more interesting hunting game.

The cat climbed high up in the tree, and seeing as he was out of reach, I preferred to let him be and go on with our game of tag. But Karl Gustav wouldn't give up. He dashed at the tree again and again. Bomba, Zuga, and Schwart encouraged him with urging barks. The poor kitten looked at Karl Gustav's sharp incisors. I could see the fear of death in his small, watery eyes. The stench of panic emanated from his small body. The pungent scent only heightened Karl Gustav's aggression and the volume of his companions' barking. Karl Gustav thrust his entire weight at the tree trunk, and the branch of safety shook beneath the cat's paws. My heart shook as well. I knew this wasn't a game. Karl Gustav was out for blood. He shot his entire body at the tree over and over, filled with boundless frustration. His paw scratched and his eyes took on a red hue of madness. It was clear that his rage would not be appeased until the poor kitten was killed.

Several young boys playing nearby got wind of the events, and decided, out of the goodness of their hearts, to lend a hand. They picked up stones and began hurling them at the cat. A direct hit threw the kitten off balance. He clawed the branch in a hopeless attempt to stabilize himself, but he quickly lost his grip and fell. Karl Gustav caught him straight from the air, and shook him fiercely.

A moment later, Karl Gustav threw the carcass away and Zuga swiftly snatched it up. He began running around proudly, as though he was the one who had made the kill. Bomba and Schwart ran after him, trying to steal his booty.

After some time, Zuga lost interest in the cat and let it drop from his mouth. The game was over and the dogs moved on to look for fresh amusement. The boys cheered and praised the hunt and the excellent hunter. Bomba, Zuga, and Schwart also received pats and praise. I glanced at the young kitten lying dead with open eyes, and distanced myself from the revelry. I knew that this time it was different. This time it wasn't just a mischievous urination on the kitchen floor or forbidden climbing on the sofas. This time I had done something really evil. I couldn't bear to look at the dead kitten. His accusing eyes made me feel deeply ashamed.

My soul sank.

Kalman and Karl Gustav's owner came and hooked us back onto our leashes. Kalman led me back home at a quickened pace. I wondered why Kalman had cut our time at the park short. Was it because he disapproved of the cat hunt? He didn't scold me or smack my snout. He must have been upset at something else. He didn't even let me linger for a moment of sniffing when Heidi and Brigitte walked by. I gave him a scathing look. *Vi got iz dir lib?* *Just a brief moment of invasive sniffing and we'll be on our way!* But Kalman pulled on the leash with some force and dragged me home. He was troubled and, to be frank, he carried the same scent that had just recently caused such calamity. Fear.

I would often hear the Gottliebs puzzle at my ability to recognize their moods and act accordingly – to rejoice with them in their happiness, to leave them be when they were busy, and to lie by their sides when they were sad. What can I say? It was an impossible feat for my feeble-nosed friends, but to me it was second nature. The scent they gave off would always reveal their temperament. People know how to fool one another and pretend they feel one way, when in fact they feel another. We dogs always know what's happening inside the human soul.

My ability to read their moods made me into a friend who would listen in times of need.

"They never buy me anything," Herschel told me. "They're so annoying! They buy Joshua every book he wants, and what am I asking for? Just a pair of soccer cleats!"

"You know," Shoshana told me, as she petted the head I rested on her knees to show solidarity, "I'd never say this to Kalman, but I'm a little glad he got fired. His colleagues there flirt day and night with their young secretaries." Though I admit I didn't understand every word she said, she exuded such a clear scent of fear of abandonment that I had no choice but to join in with a sympathy bark. Who could understand how she felt as well as I?

Kalman never needed me to share his innermost secrets. He had a close friend named Baruch Zonenfeld with whom he'd speak for hours.

"I am ashamed, filled with guilt," Kalman once told Baruch Zonenfeld over the phone. "I try to reassure Shoshana and the children. I tell them over and over that they must rid their hearts of concern – that this is all temporary and everything will be all right. . . . But what if it won't be all right? My children think I can protect them. They'll find out someday that I can shield them no better than a house of cards."

The telephone always gave me an uncomfortable feeling of dissonance. Baruch's coat smelled strongly of his dog, Kugel, so I knew that he was on his way over from the moment he turned onto our street. But how could I hear Baruch's voice so clearly as he spoke with Kalman on the phone, without being able to smell him at all?

Joshua also asked his father about the puzzling contraption. "Father, how does the telephone work? How is it possible that the voice of someone so far away can sound so close?"

Kalman's scientific answer didn't help Joshua understand, and he complained that the contraption still seemed mystical and enigmatic. The breakthrough in Joshua's ability to comprehend the secrets of the telephone came after he accidentally stepped on my tail.

"Ah!" Kalman said to his son with a twinkle in his eye. "A wonderful illustration! See how stepping on the edge of Caleb's tail evoked a series of loud barks on his other side? An action on one side generates noise at the other end of the line."

The scent of fear around the house increased over the next few days. The smell stuck to Kalman, Shoshana, and the children, and became almost too much to bear. This scent of fear put me in a vigilant state and was accompanied by a burning sensation in my nostrils. I thought I was going mad. I felt I had to stand guard: from the moment the Gottliebs would step out of their front door, they'd feel threatened – easy prey for any predator.

"We had a normal life," Kalman told his wife, "more or less. I'm not deluded. I don't claim that the *goyim* liked us. But when they hurt us, we had somewhere to go. There were authorities, there was the police, there was a court of law. . . ."

"Times have changed," Shoshana responded laconically, without elaborating.

My morning and afternoon walks were shortened. Kalman and Shoshana would ask Matilda if she would mind taking me for a walk. Matilda was inexperienced in the rules of dog-walking, and she never let me linger as long as necessary at my favorite sniffing spots.

This same feeling of tension encroached on the Shabbat meals, which used to be the height of peace and quiet. The family sat around the table and sang "*Yah Ribon Olam*, God, Master of the World" in three part harmony, and they sang with extra passion the line "God, to Whom glory and greatness belong, save Your flock from the jaws of the lion and take Your people out of exile – Your people whom You chose from all other people."

"Why doesn't God take us to Israel?" Reizel asked. Even she could sense that something was not right. "Why doesn't He perform a miracle and take us out of Germany?"

Kalman explained. "Man's eyes look up to God as a dog's eyes look up to his master. The dog knows in his heart that even if his master's actions aren't clear to him, it is clear they are good for him. Thus every man of Israel should know that even if it seems as though God has abandoned us, we must trust the mercy of heaven and hold no doubts in our heart. God has only the good of His people in mind."

"Reading those damn horoscopes again?" Kalman reproached his wife.

"Where will I find hope if not in the horoscopes?"

"Pagan nonsense!"

Shoshana waited for him to leave the room, and then shared with me the prophecies written in the constellations.

"Don't listen to him," she said. "I'll read out loud. You are a Pisces, like me. Next week, you can expect pleasant surprises. Just as everything seems dark and dreary, you will receive the news you have been waiting for. Be prepared so you do not miss the opportunity!"

Shoshana was right. The horoscope was accurate. The pleasant surprise did not tarry.

"Caleb, my friend," Kalman said to me as he read the new sign put up on the door of the Tsuzamen café. "I have wonderful news for you. No more waiting outside alone." He read me the words on the new sign: 'No entrance for dogs and Jews.'

"What can I say? Who even wants to sit in a place that won't let in dogs? Let us be on our way."

We walked on, sparing me the embarrassment of being tied to the pole. I was beside myself with happiness. I was deeply grateful to the man who had put up the sign. How wonderful! Never again would I be left tied outside as Kalman sat inside enjoying his morning cup of coffee.

CHAPTER 7

I heard footsteps in the stairwell. Three people, I told myself, listening closely to the differences in their strides. I had a feeling they were on their way to our house, but I stopped myself from barking.

Slow, deliberate knocks sounded from the other side of the door.

Matilda hurried to answer the knock and found herself, as I had guessed, in front of three people. The visitors wore uniforms that only differed from one another in the amount of metal on their chests and shoulders. Their clothes were dark, their boots heavy. They greeted her with a curt, official *"Guten tag."* The tallest one asked coldly, "Are you Mrs. Matilda Schwartzschpiln?"

"Yes," she replied, drying her hands on her apron. "How can I help you?"

The three walked into the foyer and presented Matilda with a document. The taller one added in a commanding tone, "The law doesn't permit Jews to employ housekeepers under the age of forty-five."

"These aren't *ostjuden*,"* Matilda claimed. "These are good Jews."

"Good Jews!" The tall one laughed ruthlessly. "If you want to find a good Jew, go to Dachau."

Another added, "A Jew is a Jew, and the law is the law."

The three examined her reactions in the same way Karl Gustav had examined mine when we first met, scanning her eyes for signs of rebelliousness. Matilda understood that any defiance would come at a great cost and made sure to exhibit submissiveness.

"Listen," one of them said sympathetically. "You're Aryan! You deserve more than this! Scrubbing sinks in a Jew's kitchen. . . . Don't you agree that you deserve more?"

"They really treat me well . . ." she said meekly. "And it's my job. . . ."

"Making a living is important," the third said dryly, "but purity of race is more important! And besides, you needn't worry. The Jews will compensate you."

Matilda took another moment to read through the document. It was apparent that she was perturbed and didn't know what to do.

"You must leave immediately!" the tall one said. He extended his right arm. "*Heil Hitler!*"

After the uniformed men left, Matilda handed the document to Shoshana and Kalman.

"I'm so sorry that I'm not forty-five yet," she said. "I'm so sorry."

I tried to understand the situation, but to no avail. I tilted my head, but the new angle didn't give me any new insight.

---

* Jews from Eastern Europe

Matilda took her few belongings, hugged Shoshana, and shook Kalman's hand. After she left, Kalman and Shoshana sat down for a cup of sugarless tea. They drank in silence. I could smell their profound grief and knew Matilda would never come back.

That same evening, Baruch Zonenfeld came by. He visited often to delve into conversation with Kalman and enjoy a cup of coffee and biscuits. Kalman used to call his friend *Rotes Haar*. I have no idea what the nickname means. After carefully smelling Baruch's shoes and the hemline of his pants, I detected no traces of a wife or children, but the scent of his dog Kugel clung to his clothes like a tick. Kugel was a dark dog with curly fur that hung over his forehead, slightly covering his eyes. Sometimes Kugel would join his owner when he came to visit us. I was told to receive him with open paws. I understood that they expected me to act courteously, but I can't say that I liked having another dog in the vicinity of my food dish. Every dog knows that a flagrant violation of the intimate dog-dish relationship cannot be ignored. The sudden aggression that descended on me when Kugel neared my bowl was expressed in a series of loud barks, the quivering of my upper lip, and my bared fangs.

"Caleb, calm down." Kalman kneeled at my side and stroked my head. "You are descended from Abraham's dog, and you must show hospitality, as our forefather and his canine did." Kalman spoke softly, and his words soothed me enough to allow me to watch with furious restraint as Kugel plundered my food dish.

"Coffee?" Shoshana asked.

"Gladly," said Kalman.

Baruch added, "Yes, for me too, please."

I walked Shoshana to the kitchen and back as she carried a tray with three mugs and a plate of cookies. As we entered the living room, Kalman was in the middle of a story. ". . . then who comes out to greet him but the *mikveh** lady, holding a frying pan in one hand and a rolling pin in the other, and hitting the frying pan against the rolling pin twice. Then the butcher's wife tells the rabbi, 'if you had a gold watch and you went to the *mikveh*. . . .'"

Shoshana set down the tray. "*Nu*, Kalman, that annoying joke again. You know that I don't like it when you tell crude jokes in the house, let alone ones that aren't even funny."

"Let me be, Shoshana. This isn't a crude joke and it's *extremely* funny."

"So tell it some other time. I don't like this joke."

"I'm not sure there will be another time," Baruch interjected. "As a matter of fact, I just came to say goodbye."

"Goodbye?!"

"Yes. I've decided to take a train to Italy and sail from there to Israel. Things here have become absolutely unbearable."

"Are you serious?"

"I'm completely serious. I've already paid for the tickets. One for me and one for Kugel. How could I joke about this? I've been thrown out of six work interviews already. They ask if you're a member of the party, and once they

* ritual bath

understand that you're Jewish, they won't even let you finish your sentence. You know what it's like. You're looking for a job too, aren't you?"

Kalman lowered his head. "I went to one interview. That was enough."

"So what are you living on? How can you support your family this way?"

"I think you'll eventually regret your decision," Kalman said. "Running away isn't the way to go. Yes, I agree. Things are very difficult for me and Shoshana as well. In the meantime, thank God, we still have some savings. . . . I hope it won't be necessary, but if we need to, we can sell some of the jewelry, too."

"Kalman, we have to get out of here. There's no future here. We need to get out of here before it's too late."

"It's never too late. We can always get up and leave. But running away like this is a mistake! Today it's Hitler in Germany, and tomorrow it will be somebody else somewhere else. We can't show them that if they give us a hard time, we just get up and run. My Uncle Yechiel was injured twice in the war against the French. Twice! For two months he lay in the hospital, and then he went back to the battlefield. In the end. . . ."

"In the end he got the Iron Cross, yes, I know. I've heard this story before."

"Our family, and us too," said Kalman, getting straight to the point. "We fought for this country. We can't just get up and leave."

"But Kalman, I'm telling you. This is just the beginning. Blood will be flowing in the streets."

"You're exaggerating. You've always had a flare for the

dramatic, and you're being dramatic now. It's a passing fad, a whim. Today, in order to be popular in Germany, you have to be an anti-Semite. It won't last. Look, they've even taken down the signs in the parks and stores."

"They've taken down the signs so that the foreign press won't take any pictures. When the Olympics are over, the signs will be back and things will get worse."

"The Nazi thugs can be wholly unsympathetic, I agree. But to get up and run. . . . No!"

"I'm not running because of a couple of thugs," Baruch said, looking prophetically out the window. "This time it's much more than a couple of thugs. This time it's darkness. It's darkness, Kalman! Do you understand? Darkness! A great big darkness is going to descend on our Germany. And it won't dissipate quickly. Germany has willingly cuffed itself to the devil, and will ultimately pay a grave price."

A long moment of silence pervaded the living room.

"Listen," Baruch continued. "A government emissary came by my house this morning. He made me sign a court order. There's a new law, Kalman. I have to give up Kugel within thirty days."

"Give up Kugel?"

"The decree is based on new laws – you read the paper, don't you? The Nuremburg Laws. Jews are not allowed to raise dogs."

The air in the house froze.

Shoshana lifted me onto her knees and said weakly, "If we have to give him up, the children's hearts will break."

"Enough," Kalman said. "I'm sick of talking about this."

He rose and turned on the radio.

Through the netted front of the wooden box barked a

voice that I had already learned to recognize. Hitler's voice.
I listened with them, but I could not understand a word.

"Yes," Baruch concluded. "This time Hitler has crossed
the line. I have decided to take Kugel and run. And I'm
telling you again, you should do the same."

"Look at him," Kalman nodded in my direction.

Baruch and Shoshana looked at me and smiled.

"He's listening to the radio with us," Shoshana said.

"He must be asking himself what that horrid language
is." Baruch tried to guess my thoughts. "He must think it's
just a humorless Yiddish dialect."

"Yes," Kalman agreed, petting my head softly. "Hitler's
Yiddish is indeed garbled and unclear."

Baruch smiled sadly.

Suddenly, Kugel crossed the line. I was playing harm-
lessly with an old sock that Kalman had given me, when
Kugel came with no warning and sunk his teeth into the
edge of the sock. He growled aggressively, a growl that got
louder by the moment. A growl that meant 'let go, and if
you don't – I'll bite!'

"Father!" the children called, the growls having roused
them from their rooms. "Tell them to stop!" They were
concerned that the sock tug-of-war would escalate into a
real fight.

"Children," Kalman said, as he separated me and Kugel,
"sit on the sofa, please."

He presented the confiscated sock to the children and
declared, "Whoever wins the trial will win the sock."

"I will represent Kugel," his owner said.

"And I will represent Caleb," said Kalman. "As for
Mother, well, even though she's related to one of the coun-

selors, namely me, we appoint her to preside over us on the bench."

"We will now hear the opening arguments in the Caleb vs. Kugel case," Shoshana said. "The prosecution has the floor."

Baruch Zonenfeld made a solid claim. "First of all, my client's sole intention was playing. It was Caleb who turned an innocent tug-of-war game into a dispute. Moreover, up until he took his first bite, my client had no idea that the item was a sock, let alone that there was a dog at the other end. Additionally, my client would like to note that he is well-versed in food-finding laws, and anyone who knows my client will testify that he is a law-abiding canine. It is clear that in this case he has the right to the sock."

"Well," Shoshana turned to Kalman. "What is your response?"

"I sincerely hope," Kalman said, "that my colleague's self-contradictory statements haven't confused Her Honor, and that she won't be blinded by the witty council's sharp tongue."

Shoshana smiled at Kalman, and asked him to vow in the name of his client, myself, that the sock was my own.

Kalman vowed in my name: "If I live to be a hundred and three, I'll never pee on another tree."

In the end, Her Honor Frau Gottlieb decided on joint custody. "Kugel will receive half the sock and Caleb will receive the other half."

I found the verdict abominable, but my barks of objection were overruled. Everyone celebrated the successful conclusion of a fair trial, and I alone was left feeling deceived, deprived, and betrayed.

CHAPTER 8

*O*ne morning I awoke with no appetite. I was nauseous and dizzy, and there seemed to be an elephant squatting on my chest.

"Mother," Reizel called out, concerned, "what's wrong with Caleb? Why won't he eat?"

Shoshana looked me over and replied, "He may be sick."

By the afternoon, my breaths were shallow and rattling, and my body was shaking uncontrollably.

"There are old clothes in the *boidem*," Shoshana told her children. "Wrap a shirt around him."

They wrapped the old shirt around me when they took me out for walks in the cold winter air. The improvised outfit was embarrassing and didn't protect me from the chill inside me. I lay around for three days like a lump in the living room corner. The illness raged. My breath was wheezy. An upset stomach kept me off my feet. Shoshana and Kalman brought in the vet with worried looks on their faces. Doktor Richard Hess announced that my days were numbered. The diagnosis: a severe nasal infection and a swollen liver. He took a syringe out of his bag and recommended putting me down. Shoshana and Kalman considered his suggestion with utmost seriousness, but Herschel wouldn't hear of it. That night, nightmare followed nightmare. I saw my late brother, the moment his head dropped for the final time. I feared that my head would soon drop with the same finality, never to rise again. Sleep scared me. What if my soul He would not keep?

I heard a voice.

It sounded as though Kalman was calling me, and I walked over to Shoshana and Kalman's bedroom, only to find a closed door. I could hear Kalman's snores, Shoshana's deep breaths.

I returned to my corner and heard the voice call my name again.

I wandered from room to room, but everyone was fast asleep. Back on my rug, I could feel all my limbs succumbing to exhaustion. I fell into a deep sleep. In my vision, I heard the voice say:

"Fear not, Caleb. I am thy protector, and your reward shall be great."

"Must this come right before I die?" I asked in my dream.

The voice in the dream granted me but one wish. **"What shall I give you?"**

And I spake, "I am but a small pup, and I know not the ways of life. If You may, please grant Your servant a heart that understands the speech of man."

And He said to me, **"As you have asked for this, and you asked not for steaks or wieners, and you asked not for vengeance against thine enemies, I will grant your wish. I shall give you a wise and understanding heart** so that there never was, nor will there ever be, anyone like you – a dog among dogs for all time. And I will give unto your offspring this land, and the Canaanite, and the Dalmatian, and the Saluki, from the river of Egypt to. . . ."

I awoke.

There was no one around me, but I could practically reach out my paw and touch the voice that had spoken. I stared into the darkness until I fell asleep once more. At the break of dawn, Herschel came and pried my jaws open. He used a syringe to squirt chicken soup and sugar water into my mouth. The forced feeding strengthened me and I thanked him with a single lick. He faithfully administered liquids several times a day. Slowly, his efforts paid off. Within a few days, I was able to eat on my own. From that moment, I swore to follow Herschel wherever he went. I wouldn't leave him alone for a moment. I knew that without his adamant objection to the doctor's recommendation and but for his undying devotion, I would be. . . .

In the days that Herschel nursed me on my sickbed, there was a general gloominess in the air. Dinners were chewed in silence, and this silence was rarely broken.

"Were you at the Ministry of the Interior today?" Shoshana asked, "Did you take care of the name changes?"

Kalman responded with a curt nod and placed five booklets on the table.

"Sarah and Israel." Shoshana examined the booklets. "Just like your parents."

"You should have seen the clerk. She had this sign above her, 'Head of Jewish Passport Department.' She was a typical cold bureaucrat, and wore as much makeup as a call-girl. You would think she was doing us a favor. And you wouldn't believe the fee they charged for it!"

"So do we have to call Reizel 'Sarah' now?" Herschel asked.

"And you're Israel from now on," Reizel retorted, sticking her tongue out.

"Enough with the rubbish," Kalman ruled. "We needn't change a thing!"

And Joshua said, "Only Caleb gets to stay Caleb."

CHAPTER 9

I was sitting at Kalman's feet in the living room. The children had already gone out, book-bags on their backs. Shoshana had departed with a basket. Several times a week, she would leave with an empty basket, always to return with the basket brimming with goodies. I had no idea how she did it.

Suddenly, the doorknob turned and the door opened.

The guests hadn't bothered to knock, and being familiar with human etiquette, I could tell that something was wrong. *Intruders!* I said to myself. The hairs on my nape stood on end. I pulled my ears back and barked, baring my fangs. I could hear my jaws snapping together between each bark. I tensed all my muscles and I was ready to bite. I was even ready to be struck. The meaning of my barks was clear: back off or I'll attack.

One of them took a greyish silver object out of his pocket. Kalman leapt from his seat and stood between me and the intruders. He grabbed my collar firmly and lifted me until my front paws were off the ground.

"Quiet, Caleb! Quiet!" Kalman ordered me. "No! Stupid dog! No barking!"

Kalman looked anxiously at the two men who had invaded his home.

The shiny object was returned to the man's pocket.

"We're here to make a property appraisal," said the man, who was short and stout. He took two steps forward, his folds of fat following close behind. He and his friend walked between the rooms, holding notepads. Kalman wouldn't let go of my collar the entire time they were there. He heard the furious grunts coming from my throat, muted but ready to burst out at any moment, and held me tight. "No, Caleb," he said. "Quiet. No barking."

I knew that Kalman was not happy to see these guests. I could sense that he felt threatened, and I wanted to chase away the source of danger with a bark and a bite. I wanted Kalman to know that I would give my life for him, but I remained silent.

Kalman could see I understood that it was best to remain silent, and petted the back of my neck softly.

"Good dog," he said. "Good dog."

When the two finally left, I began barking loudly. Kalman came up to me once again, calming me with a pat, and whispering in my ear.

"Yes, my sparrow.

Yes, my chick.

Yes, my lark.

Yes, now you can bark."

Shoshana returned and placed the basket of food on the table. She was holding a letter.

"Don't ask," she told Kalman, her voice strung with frustration. "I stood in line for two hours, and in the end they didn't even have any. . . ." She glanced at Kalman and saw in his expression that something was wrong. "Are you all right?" she asked. "Did something happen?"

"Two pencil pushers came by. I'm glad you weren't here. They came to get a property appraisal. One of them almost shot Caleb."

Shoshana froze. "Brutes!"

"Scum of the earth," Kalman confirmed. "One dwarf with glasses and a porcupine haircut who wouldn't let go of his ballpoint pen for a second, and the other a skinny 'four-eyes' with an evil glare and a jumpy Adam's apple. You should have seen how they walked around the house as though they owned it all. And their ever-so-witty comments. 'I've never seen rats raising a dog.' I hope those damn National Socialists burn in hell!"

"Thank God they didn't hurt Caleb."

"Caleb is a smart dog," Kalman said. "It's unbelievable. He understood that he needed to sit quietly. He acted as though he really understood everything. Like a human."

Then he looked at the letter in her hand. "And what came in the mail?"

"Herr Buchwald, the school principal, would like to meet with us," Shoshana reported. "It's probably about a certain note of a romantic nature that the literature teacher intercepted during class."

Kalman took his wife's hand in his own. "I was sure the teacher would want to punish Joshua for passing notes in class. Who would have thought that he would recommend to the principal to cultivate our young, budding poet?"

"Well," Shoshana said with a smile, "he certainly didn't get his talent from me."

Kalman smiled back. "At least one of my children is following in my footsteps. I started writing at that age myself. My mother saved a handful of things I wrote. I need to ask her where she keeps my manuscripts. That is, if she still remembers."

"I find it hard to believe that she saved them," Shoshana let go of her husband's hand. "You know how she cleans for Passover. Plenty of gems have found their way into the wastebasket."

Kalman responded with a sigh of agreement.

"Did you write as nicely as Joshua?" Shoshana asked.

Kalman hesitated for a moment. "No. If I recall correctly, at his age I couldn't rhyme half as well as he. Though I did first find love at that age. . . ."

"Yes, yes," Shoshana said hurriedly. "So we've heard."

CHAPTER 10

Kalman came home when the rest of the family was already in the middle of dinner. He had a sour look on his face, and his presence filled the room with tension. I knew it was a bad time to beg for leftovers.

"The meeting was unsuccessful?" Shoshana asked.

"Fifty minutes he kept me waiting," Kalman said as he removed his coat. "Fifty minutes, and in the end I was barely in his office for five. You should have seen the pictures he has hanging on the wall across from the waiting area. Faces and profiles of various races, with a list of characteristics. We're not portrayed in the best way, no surprise there. . . ."

"What did he say about me?" Joshua wanted to know.

Shoshana also asked, "What did he say about Joshua?"

"He didn't call me in to discuss his literary talent. He called me in to relay a message. I'm afraid that it's not good news. He learned that Joshua had been passing a flirtatious note to his classmate. 'Astrid Lingenmaier is the daughter of an SS officer, therefore the disgrace is doubly inexcusable. For the benefit of all the parties . . .' so he said, 'it has been decided that Joshua, Reizel, and Herschel will not attend school anymore.'"

"What does that mean? We'll never ever go back to school?" Herschel asked.

"I don't know," his father replied, unable to meet his eyes.

"And if I go back next year, will I be in second grade again, or can I continue with my friends in third grade?" Reizel asked.

Kalman and Shoshana exchanged glances and didn't answer.

"I don't like school anyway," Herschel declared. "I don't even mind staying home."

Kalman gave him a look and Herschel fell silent.

"In other news," Kalman said, "I ran into Baruch. He said there are rumors that prisoners in the labor camps have been instructed to sew yellow Stars of David onto prison uniforms."

"What does that mean?" Joshua asked.

"It's possible," Kalman said, "that the evil Hitlerites have plans to imprison Jews and have them do manual labor."

"Pharaoh had us do manual labor too," Reizel recalled. "Why does everyone make us do manual labor?"

"I don't know why," Shoshana admitted. "But I do know what the end of all the evil people will be. Do you remember what happened to Pharaoh and the Egyptians?"

"God punished them – He smote them with ten plagues and then cast them into the sea."

"That's right," Joshua said. "God punished Pharaoh and the Egyptians, and He'll punish Hitler, may his name be blotted out, and all his Nazi cronies."

"Look," Herschel said, pointing at me. "Every time we're sad, Caleb is sad too."

"Look how he's lying there," Shoshana said, "with those droopy ears. He's really empathizing with us."

"And if we're happy, will he be happy with us?"

"Of course!" Herschel cried, and stood, clapping and rejoicing. I rose with him, wagging my tail and barking joyously. Herschel smirked, his point proven.

After these things had come to pass, Kalman hooked the leash to my collar, apparently hoping that an evening walk would calm his spirits. We walked at the same pace, leaving my leash limp. Kalman was lost in his thoughts. I tried to guess what was going on in his head, but I was soon distracted by the urine messages left by my friends on the lampposts, walls, and trees we passed: Spitz was claiming the title of dominant male of south-west Stuttgart, Heidi was spreading the news that she had begun to discover her sexuality, and a new dog, old and sick, had joined the neighborhood.

I could hear barks and cheers coming from the direction of the Rosenpark, drawing my attention. I glanced at Kalman, who looked curious as well. I shot forward, stretching my leash. I said to myself, *I shall go down and see what is the matter.* Kalman was dragged in my footsteps to see what was going on. In the center of a circle of spectators and curiosity-seekers, Karl Gustav and a Rottweiler female were busy getting busy. The owners of the two dogs, like the rest of the onlookers, were encouraging the couple.

"Look," Karl Gustav's hunchbacked owner said, presenting documents to Kalman. "Karl Gustav is the epitome of Rottweiler purity. These documents present his spotless pedigree, all the way back to the forefathers of the Rottweiler dynasty. His mate has certificates, too. A German Rottweiler champion."

Kalman faked a look of enthusiasm so as not to damper the proud father's excitement. I surprised even myself with my ability to notice such subtleties in human behavior.

"This is no regular pairing up," the hunched German said. "This is eugenics." Excited by the thought, he added with verve, "Behold, a daring and ruling race rises. . . ."

Karl Gustav climbed with his upper body onto the female, who was giving off a scent that made me feel naked. He squeezed her hips with his hind legs and moved his rump with lustful convulsions. A pink and fleshy carrot emerged from its hiding place and poked out between his legs. The female barked and whimpered, excited and nervous. I watched them with great interest, virginal and embarrassed to the bone. A disorienting tickling sensation swept through my loins. Kalman pulled me back. I tried to anchor my legs to the ground, but Kalman was too strong as he said with a fatherly tone, "Come, Caleb, come. You're still too young for such sights."

In the middle of the night, I heard voices coming from Shoshana and Kalman's room. I went to lie down at their door.

"What's on your mind?" I heard Shoshana ask her husband. "Why can't you sleep?"

"It's eating me up inside, I can't stop thinking about it.

Somehow I kept denying it. I can't believe that they would make us give up the dogs." His voice cracked. "How can we give them away? It's almost like giving away children. You know how hard it will be to find them a good home. Caleb is so attached to Bruriah, and she's so attached to him. . . . It'll be a crime to separate them."

"We need to be realistic," Shoshana said. "We're not going to find anyone who will agree to adopt them both, certainly not within a month. Matilda loved Bruriah very much. I'll talk to her tomorrow morning. I think she may agree to adopt her."

"All right," Kalman tried to joke. "It's only fair that Matilda find a home for Bruriah, since Bruriah and her puppies were devoted to creating so much filth, thereby ensuring a full time job for a fine daughter of the German people, who, as you know, cherish work above all else."

Shoshana didn't respond.

"I really hope they retract that damn law."

"I went to a pawnshop today," Shoshana changed the subject. "I asked how much we can get for the candlesticks and the watches."

"Forget it! That's not on the table right now. At this point, we aren't pawning a thing."

"You needn't be angry. I just wanted to find out how much the things are worth. You know, just in case. . . ."

They fell asleep, and so did I. But the dark of the night was nothing compared to the dark day I was to wake up to in mere hours.

CHAPTER 11

Kalman went over to the telephone and turned the dial several times.

"Bruriah isn't a puppy," he explained to the phone. "She's completely house trained and only relieves herself outside. Financially, she'll be no burden at all. I promise to pay for her food expenses for the entire year."

Mother, who was listening to the conversation along with the rest of us, looked at me with doleful eyes. I assume that, like me, Mother understood almost every word.

"They're on their way," Kalman announced, setting down the receiver. "She's coming with her husband."

Shoshana arranged the chairs around the table, setting everything perfectly in place. She put out some refreshments. Mother and I knew that we were forbidden to taste the food. My mother came close to me. If I could translate the rubbing of her neck against mine and the slow licking of her tongue on my face into human talk, it would read something like this: Take care, my little pup. I hope we will see each other again.

We cuddled together one last time.

The time passed too quickly. I tried to make the most of every moment, to imprint in my heart the feeling of Mother's large paws, the roughness of her tongue, the loving look in her eye, her grief. I closed my eyes, trying to absorb the experience in its entirety. And then, through my closed eyes, for a moment, just a split second, a blink of the eye, I saw a vision. Her paw held a piece of chalk and was writing on the wall:

Werd ich zum Augenblicke sagen:
Verweile doch du bist schön
Dann magst du mich in Fesseln schlagen
Dann will ich gern zugrunde gehen!

If ever I to the moment shall say:
beautiful moment, do not pass away!
Then you may tie your leash to bind me,
then I will put my life behind me.

Hesitant knocks on the door announced the guests we were apprehensively anticipating. Matilda stood in the doorway, a strained smile on her face and her husband at her side. He was a short man, with glasses set low on his nose and a strand of hair hanging down his forehead.

"Come on in," Shoshana said, motioning with her arm.

"This is my husband, Gabriel." Matilda introduced her companion and walked with him toward the living room.

"Hello, Herr Schwartzschpiln," Shoshana and Kalman greeted him.

I was a little surprised. The human counterpart to hind-sniffing was supposed to be hand-shaking. Now they sufficed with a curt nod of the head.

Following Shoshana and Kalman's lead, my mother and I refrained from excessive leaps of joy. Some situations, so I've discovered, require restraint and discipline.

Herr Schwartzschpiln looked around the house, nodding his head as though trying to assess the value of the property. Matilda called Mother's name, and she subsequently stood tall, showing off the full power of her Caucasian prowess.

"Nice dog," the husband said, nodding his head.

"I told you so!" Matilda said.

"And what does this name, Bruriah, mean?" he inquired.

"It's just a name . . ." Shoshana said. "It means that she's a very smart dog."

Herr Schwartzschpiln nodded. He interrogated Shoshana and Kalman about my mother's pedigree and the virtues of her breed. He seemed pleased.

"I think I know a family who has a male dog of the exact same breed. . . ."

Within a few short minutes, my mother was already on her way to the Schwartzschpiln home.

She didn't bark.

Who knows what lurks in the heart of a Hebrew canine?

CHAPTER 12

*O*ver the next few days, I was more irritable than usual.
"I think he misses his mother," Shoshana said.
"Yes," Kalman agreed. "He must understand that he's next in line."

Herschel smothered me with love, but it was mixed with anxiety over our looming separation. One morning, a Friday judging by the scents coming from Shoshana's kitchen, Herschel dragged me to the washroom and scrubbed me thoroughly with a rag soaked in scented soap. Reizel dried me off and combed my fur. I didn't enjoy being washed and groomed, but it was clear to me that I should try not to shake the water out, as it would interrupt their work and simply prolong the torture. When the children completed their masterpiece, their parents handed them their due pay and sent them off to the store.

"Buy some sweets and chocolate. Buy whatever you want."

The children didn't need any more encouragement than that, and their hurried steps soon faded down the busy street. Just a moment after their footfalls had subsided, a wary knock was heard at the door.

"Ah, right on time. Come on in," Kalman greeted the new arrival. "Tell me, what's new at the newspaper?"

The guest was Frank Heinz. Back in the day, when Kalman would leave the house early in the morning and not return until evening, Frank would often visit our home. Ever since Kalman began spending his days at home, Frank had stopped gracing us with his presence. I liked him a lot; he would always dedicate a moment of his time to me, petting me vigorously, and treating me to a delicacy the likes of which I never saw in Shoshana's kitchen: a pink-brown tail, curly with a chewy and wonderful texture and a heavenly flavor.

"So here's the little bandit," Frank said to me, petting the top of my head.

I lay on my side, lifting my right paw and exposing my underbelly for him to pet.

"My my, you smell so good. You had a bath, did you, little bandit? Greta will love him. I'm sure she'll fall for him at first sight. Our little Abarax looked just like him."

Shoshana served cookies and lemonade.

"He's a wonderful dog," she said. "A really wonderful dog."

"What can he do? Have you trained him?"

"He only knows 'sit' and 'down,' but he's very bright. When he's hungry, he'll tap his paw on the rim of his food dish, and if he wants to be taken out for a walk, he'll bring us his leash in his mouth."

"Is that so?" Frank smiled. "It sounds like the little bandit is trying to train *you*."

Kalman nodded in consent.

"Is everything all right?" Frank asked. "You seem nervous."

"I'm worried that the children will return. . . ."

"The children?! Aren't they at school?"

Kalman shook his head, and an uncomfortable silence ensued.

"Okay," Frank said. "I'll take him and go. Please don't worry, we'll treat him like a prince. We'll replace his water every day and give him plenty of food. I promise. You really mustn't worry. He'll want for nothing."

Frank rose, took my leash, and hooked it to my collar.

Kalman brought my face close to his and I could see tears in his eyes.

"Good-bye, beloved little pup. Don't you worry. Frank and his wife will treat you well."

I licked his face.

"I haven't told the children yet," he disclosed to me in a whisper. "Maybe I'll tell them that you got lost or got run over by a car. Or maybe I'll tell them the truth. I don't know what to do." Kalman took my head into his hands and blessed, "May the Lord bless you and keep you; May the Lord make His face shine light upon you and be gracious unto you; May the Lord turn His face toward you and give you peace." He held his face against mine, and his tears soaked my whiskers.

Shoshana couldn't hold her tears back either.

Frank looked embarrassed.

"You should know," she said, "he really is a very smart dog. He's like a child. It's as if he was human. He simply understands everything. He has incredible comprehension.

You really don't need to train him – he understands everything on his own."

"He looks clever . . ." Frank Heinz stammered. "You can come visit him whenever you please."

Kalman and Shoshana said nothing.

With the helplessness of a dog living in a world ruled by humans, I looked out the window of Frank's Volkswagen and stared at the Gottliebs' house for the last time.

Shoshana and Kalman watched me leave from the window. Kalman's hand held Shoshana's hip comfortingly. They both stood with their heads hanging low. How can I bear to watch these evils come upon me? How can I bear to watch the loss of my childhood home? My entire existence had been filled with Gottliebs. The air in my lungs had always been blended with their scent. What would become of me now?

I couldn't picture the world at large, let alone my own little world, without the presence of Kalman, Shoshana, and their children.

And what is such a world?

A dried ravine, an arid lake, a wasteland.

CHAPTER 13

Frank Heinz did not keep his promise. The treatment I received was despicable. From the moment I stepped into their house, Greta was decidedly cold to me. I was not granted even one hour of grace.

"Do you remember what my father said when I told him we were getting married?" she cross-examined her husband.

"I assume that's a rhetorical question."

"No, I'm really asking if you remember."

"He said I'm a good guy."

"He said: 'Frank is a good guy, but he doesn't look before he leaps.' You got mad at my father, but I'm sorry, he was one hundred percent on the mark. If you had thought about it, if you had taken five minutes to think about it, you wouldn't have done something so stupid."

"Why is this so stupid? When I brought Abarax home, you weren't over the moon at first, but it soon grew into true love."

"That's not true! With Abarax it was love at first sight. I just wasn't sure that it was the right time in our lives to raise a dog."

"And now isn't the right time?"

"What are you talking about?! It isn't about timing. How can you be so thick? The water in Abarax's dish is still clean, and you come home with a new dog? Besides, he doesn't look a thing like Abarax. How could you even think that a Jew's dog could fill Abarax's collar? What's this thing's name, anyhow?"

"Caleb."

"That's a stupid name."

"Yes, yes, of course. But names can be changed," he said, and then added jokingly, "the Jews have gotten used to their names being changed. I thought perhaps we could name him Abarax."

"What?! What?!" Greta roared.

"I'm sorry, I just thought that. . . . Well, it doesn't matter, you're right. No, it's really not a good idea. Maybe . . ." Frank suggested, trying to appease his wife. "Maybe we'll just call him Zelig. Zelig is an excellent name for a dog. Yes, it has a nice ring to it: Greta, Frank, and Zelig Heinz."

Greta walked off toward the kitchen and returned with a glass of water. She was tall and stiff. Her long strides exuded vulgarity. It was the first time in my life that I had disliked a person so intensely.

"Zelig is a nice name," she said, "but I don't have the patience or the inclination to raise this dog. I have a bad feeling about him. Look at him, he has the eyes of a Jew. I'm telling you, he isn't fit to lick Abarax's paw."

She looked at me, then at Frank, and then back at me, straightened the tablecloth and declared: "I do not want him. Either you return him to the Jewish dump he came from, or you raise him yourself!"

I listened to this humiliation with drooped ears and prayed that Frank would return me to the Jewish dump I came from.

My prayer was not answered. Frank decided to try and raise me himself. I can only assume he hoped that, as time passed, his hag of a wife would soften up and eventually accept me.

Food and walks were now cut down to a bare minimum. Once a day, Frank would fill my dish with rice and dried sausages. By my snout, I swear those moments when he filled my dish were the only happy moments of each long day. Aside from the dish-filling, I had nothing to look forward to. The food tasted fine, but the quantity left much to be desired. Every day, I waited for Frank to pick up the serving cup and go out to the balcony. The food would soon be devoured, and I would collapse onto my rug, trying to accept the fact that there were now twenty-four hours between me and my next meal. Begging for food during their meals was strictly forbidden. Where was my beloved Herschel, *zu lengere yaren*,* to stretch his hand under the table and smuggle me a bite of smoked salmon or half a butter sandwich? Once Herschel had snuck me a whole cutlet and the entire maneuver went unnoticed. I had quietly snatched the loot and gobbled it up where no one would see me. The sharp memories pierced my heart. Look at me now, I thought, my heart aching – *a ris in hertzen*.**

Each day, I was granted one walk. Two if I was lucky.

---

* he should live long
** a hole in my heart

Either way, they were never very long. Usually Frank took me out, but one of the rare instances that Greta walked me was brutally eye-opening. She dragged me along at a quickened pace that didn't allow for my customary sniffing breaks. Then she met one of her friends. The friend wasn't quite as tall as Greta, but she was a sizeable woman, wrapped in a fur stole and holding a cigarette between two long fingers. A smile stretched over her powdered face. "Ah, how nice. I didn't know you adopted a new dog."

"Please, do not even joke about that. I intend to get rid of this dog the first chance I have."

"He's actually pretty cute. What did he do to get on your bad side?"

"I don't think he's cute at all. He sits in the corner and does nothing all day. If we leave him home alone, he wreaks havoc. Last week, he ate half of my living room carpet."

"I don't see anything wrong with sitting in the corner," Powder Lady said. "I wish my Shtinky would just sit quietly sometimes and not wag his tail all over the house, knocking glasses off the table. . . . By the way, I read Frank's last interview with Piet Harlan. I must say I simply loved it. To tell you the truth, I didn't even know that Christina Söderbaum was his wife. How is dear Frank?"

"Frank is fine. He mentioned recently that he might be asked to write about Carl Orff, but I don't know much more than that. He hasn't done much since his last article, besides bringing this pest into our home. . . ."

"Listen, I have an idea for you. You can buy him a chew bone at the butcher. He'll be too busy with the bone to cause too much harm."

"I'll think about it," Greta said, and the two parted.

And I, understanding almost every word despite the strange pronunciation, didn't know what to do with myself. There was the vague promise of a bone, but Greta's cold words laid out the harsh reality clearly for me. It was a painful blow. I suddenly realized how far I'd fallen. In one swift motion, I went from pet to pest.

On our way home, we walked past a large park. Many dogs were playing together there. I barked, indicating that I wanted to play with them. I wagged my tail in the most sycophantic manner, but Greta was not impressed, and I was dragged back home against my will. I was frustrated, and refused to subdue my playfulness. My usual way to generate some excitement and fun was to tear paper. I took a book that had been placed within jaws' reach and shook it so hard that half the pages fell out. I was so engrossed in the shredding that I barely noticed Greta, the killjoy, entering the room.

"No!" she cried. "Not *Mein Kampf!* This time you've gone too far!"

She locked me in the pantry. Outside, it was getting dark and I started to worry. I didn't know if my punishment had a time limit. This was the first time in my life that an unsurmountable obstacle stood between me and my water dish. It was the first time in my life that a door separated me from my food bowl. I sat on a rag and rested my head on my paws. What would happen when I'd need to empty my bladder?

I heard knocks on the front door and Greta's clicking heels hurrying over to open it. The key turned. I hoped it would be Frank, but instead I heard the sincere voice of Father Flaschbuch.

"Say 'Good evening' to Mrs. Heinz," he instructed his daughter.

"Good evening," said the well-trained Barbara.

Greta reciprocated with a greeting of her own.

From the pantry, I could hear Greta reading to little Barbara from their usual book.

At first I listened carefully to Greta and to her stories, but eventually I lost interest. Time ticked away slowly until I suddenly heard Frank's footsteps in the hallway. He walked into the house.

I considered barking, or at least emitting a weak whimper, but Frank, who was obviously surprised not to find me jumping on him as usual, beat me to the chase and asked his wife, "Where is Zelig?"

They began to argue.

"What?!" Frank sounded appalled. "You haven't taken him out? He's been locked in the pantry since this morning?"

"He could burst in there, for all I care!" Greta yelled. "A sorry excuse for a dog!"

Barbara began to cry, and the shouting subsided. Frank let me out of the pantry and hooked on my leash. I loved my leash; it still smelled of Kalman.

"You can stop by the butcher and get him a bone," Greta suggested before our departure. "Maybe if he has something to chew on, he won't cause quite as much trouble."

"Yes," Frank replied. "Yes, that's a good idea. I'm sorry I raised my voice at you. . . ."

We went on our walk. Something in the air told me that it was almost the Sabbath. My nostrils were tickled by the familiarity of distant scents. Frank and Greta had no traditional family meal. They didn't light candles or recite a blessing after washing their hands. They didn't sing throughout the meal, nor did they mumble to themselves at its close. Instead, at the beginning of each meal, Greta would hold her hands together, bow her head, and say Grace to her Savior. She would then move one hand up and down and side to side before beginning to eat.

Outside, we met Maximilian sitting on the bench, waiting. Frank sat by his side and let out a long sigh. "That woman is nothing but trouble," he said. "She just won't let me be. She always reminds me of what her father used to say." Then he imitated her high-pitched, argumentative voice, "Frank is a good boy, but he leaps before he looks."

"He couldn't be more right!" Maximilian said, resting a comforting arm on Frank's shoulder. "If you had given it a moment of thought, you wouldn't have married the daughter of such a pain in the ass."

Maximilian was a charming man with a square and lanky build. His facial features were refined, and a long cigarette was permanently fixed in his mouth.

Frank looked at Maximilian and nodded. Then he hid his face in his hands and let out a long breath. "She treats Zelig worse than you could imagine. Today she had him locked up in the pantry all day."

"The monster!" Maximilian was shocked. "My word, she's simply a monster! You have to leave that woman."

"Yes, and then spend the rest of my life broke. . . ."

"You're addicted to whining!" Maximilian didn't spare him. "A journalist who writes about Piet Harlan and Carl Orff won't have to beg for money, and you know plenty well that I'd never let you spend a night on the streets. But what can I say? It's your life."

After a moment of silence, their eyes met. "Shall we go up for a cup of coffee?"

Frank made a face and shook his head. "She's home, as usual, watching the minister's dim-witted daughter."

"Father Flaschbuch's?"

"Yes. Reading her the stories of Christ over and over. Even Zelig would get bored listening to those stories so many times."

Maximilian patted my head and spoke directly to me. "Jesus, the protagonist of the New Testament, was one of you guys. Yes, as a young man, he was part of your Jewish pack, until he got sick of them and started his own pack. His new pack was extremely popular and new members began joining at a dizzying rate. And shall I tell you another fascinating tidbit, my furry little friend? Jesus was blessed with especially low density. . . ."

Frank gave him a quizzical look.

"It helped him walk across some ponds."

Frank smiled affectionately at his friend and said, "Stop being an idiot."

"If Greta is allowed, so am I," Maximilian responded. "Jesus had amazing healing powers. He was a supervet. Every lame dog he met suddenly stopped limping, and every docked cocker spaniel he petted resprouted his tail. Blind dogs could see again, and anosmic dogs could smell again. And do you want to hear one more secret?" He looked at me and then at Frank. It had been so long since I had received such attention, and I barked happily. "Jesus was God's son, but to bring him into the world He didn't even have to have. . . ."

"Enough nonsense!" Frank scolded Maximilian. "I need to get back home and buy a bone for Zelig on the way. I should hurry. You know what Greta is like. She'll start getting suspicious. . . ."

CHAPTER 14

The first thought that went through my mind the moment my paws touched the rug in Frank and Greta's house was that I must escape. But after receiving three angry spanks from Greta, it was no longer a thought. It was an existential feeling that took hold of me.

It all began with the damned bone that Frank bought at the butcher.

"Here," Greta said, holding the bone in front of my snout. "This is for you. Eat it and enjoy – just don't come near the carpets."

I accepted the gift, and had she not moved her hand away in the blink of an eye, I would have thanked her with a lick. Excellent! We had now turned over a new leaf in our relationship. I chewed the bone thoroughly and with great care, milking every drop of juicy marrow. After a long hour of chewing, I grew tired and satisfied, and I decided to hide my bone in a safe location. I noticed a lump in the sofa and dug my teeth in. Before long, I had created a small hollow in the cushion for the bone. I knew it would be safe there.

I didn't want to lose the bone as it represented a positive turn in my relationship with Greta.

When Greta came home, she began screaming like a madwoman at the sight of the living room.

"You idiot! Idiot!" she cried. She picked up a slipper and started hitting me. "Bad dog! Bad! Bad dog!"

I cried soundlessly, and a horrible feeling urging me to escape this dungeon filled my heart.

Weeks went by and the feeling wouldn't pass. In fact, it grew stronger every day. I must return to the Gottliebs, come what may. As I lay in my corner at night, I tried to find an explanation. Against whom had I sinned to deserve such a punishment? Did the Gottliebs take insult in my mischievous deeds? Did I bark too much?

I recalled my role in the cat hunt. The image of the limp corpse resurfaced in my mind. Indeed, I was being punished. I accepted my stay at Frank and Greta's as fair judgment. At night I was haunted by the kitten's accusing eyes, and I slept restlessly.

Though I accepted my fate, my remorse did not last long. Though I knew I deserved the punishment, I made a firm decision not to bear it. I would seize the first opportunity and make my escape. Two months later, I was granted the perfect opening. Because the damage I had caused to the sofa was irreparable, the Heinzes decided to purchase a new couch. The old one was taken down to the street and a group of porters carried up the new one. Greta and Frank hovered around the porters to ensure that the doorposts weren't damaged. I took advantage of the hustle and bustle, and snuck out. I managed to cross a mere two blocks when the sky went dark and rain came pouring down from the heavens. To my sensitive ears, the thunder sounded like the trumpets of the apocalypse. I ran frantically to the nearest shelter I could think of – Frank and Greta's house.

"Ah, here you are," Frank said happily. "I was wondering where you'd disappeared to."

"And I don't understand why you came back," Greta muttered just loud enough for Frank to hear.

"Why are you so hostile?" Frank asked. "You know, Shoshana said. . . ."

"Who is Shoshana?"

"Frau Gottlieb, Kalman's wife. Shoshana said that he's a very bright dog. She said that he has an extraordinary grasp of things."

"I don't think he can even grasp his own tail."

Her cruel comeback was followed by a strike of lightning and clap of thunder. The noise was terrifying. As quickly as I could, before the lightning would turn me into a lump of coal, I took cover under the table. Greta saw how frightened I was and burst into laughter that dripped with scorn. She pointed at me and said, "Here's your genius dog. Look at him, hiding like a nincompoop. Look at your cowardly Jew dog. Look how he's shivering from a few claps of thunder."

She liked the new nickname she dubbed me with – "Jew dog" – and wouldn't stop using it. It was always accompanied by degrading adjectives: "Come here, you filthy Jew dog." "Tell the stupid Jew dog to stop barking," "Look how that flea-ridden Jew dog you brought in can't stop scratching himself."

The initial hostility I had felt toward Greta developed into complete abhorrence. My world became gray and bitter. I became depressed, my appetite diminished, and I lost weight. I couldn't remember the last time I had wagged my tail.

I was furious at myself for being such a coward, and swore that I would not squander my next opportunity for freedom.

CHAPTER 15

*I*ntense doubts gnawed at me day and night, but I stayed strong. Although my attempt to escape had failed, I would not accept such a fate. I would not serve a life sentence with the submissive Frank and his witch of a wife. But what could I do?

How would I free myself from Greta's evil clutches? When would there be another chance to flee?

It was Greta, of all people, who opened the window of opportunity. She would often accuse her husband of bringing a dismal dog into the house. Not once did it cross her mind that she herself was the cause of my gloom. Frank apologized time and time again, embarrassed. "I really don't know what happened. At the Gottliebs he always seemed so joyful and vivacious. Maybe he's ill."

I was taken to the vet for a full examination. His name was Marzel, and he gave off a Jewish scent that reminded me of home. Honey, horseradish, old books, and garlic. He had a private clinic adjacent to his home. The nostalgia induced by the Jewish aroma got my tail wagging energetically.

Doktor Marzel Cohen probed my inner organs, making sure they were all set in their proper place. He held my mouth open and looked inside, checked my pupils, examined my ears, and scrutinized the mercury thermometer that he inserted in my *tuches*.

"Your dog is perfectly healthy," he ceremoniously announced, and undercharged Frank for the visit due to lack of findings.

"Well, how do you explain that he sits around the house all day, as still as a statue?"

"A dog needs company, Frank my friend. He needs time to run and play with other dogs. He needs children to throw sticks for him to fetch. Your kids have all grown up and moved away, and I presume a busy newspaper man such as yourself doesn't have the time to care for the cute little puppy."

"All right," Frank said, and thanked the vet for the exam. "I'll think of a way to try to give him some more of my time."

"You have to. Otherwise the poor thing will die of grief."

I had been listening closely to the vet, and I was moved by his precise diagnosis.

On our way home, we passed by a large grassy field. A schnauzer with a trowel-shaped snout barked at me from the other side of the road. Frank recognized the golden-haired lady holding the schnauzer's leash.

We crossed the street.

"Hello, Paula. What's new at the newspaper?

"Hello, Herr Frank. Not much is happening by us. Why don't we let the dogs run around on the grass for a while?"

Frank hesitated and Paula urged him to stay. "Just for a few minutes. It's good for them. Look how happy Leopold is to meet friends. He's not aggressive. There's really nothing to worry about."

"No, that's not the issue. . . ."

Paula leaned toward me. "What's your name, cutie?"

Leopold stood on his hind legs and let out a string of jealous barks.

"His name is Zelig," Frank answered for me. He glanced at his watch. "If I'm late for dinner, Greta won't let me hear the end of it."

I wagged my tail and barked enthusiastically. It had been ages since I last met a nice dog to share a short game of tag with. Frank looked at me encouragingly, Doktor Marzel's advice echoing in his ears. "Oh, all right. But just for a few minutes."

Round-faced Paula and Frank brought us closer to one another. We stood for a moment, Leopold and I, in the conventional mutual sniffing position. I got the impression that we could play together without fear of our game turning sour. On the one hand, he seemed calm and secure, while on the other hand, he seemed to lack the compulsion to control and dominate. The sight of my wagging tail and Leopold's cheerfully oscillating stump convinced our owners that they need not fear, and they released us from our leashes.

I crouched down, extended my front paws, and held them close to the grass. My tail went straight up into the air, declaring *if you chase me, I'll run like the wind*. Leopold accepted my challenge, and I began evasive maneuvers, leaving a confused schnauzer on my trail. Out of the corner of my eye, I saw Frank engrossed in conversation with the young lady, his eyes off me. Now! This is my chance! I would be a neglected and lonely dog no more. I must find my way back to the Gottliebs. My heart was flooded with a wave of yearning for the feeling of Reizel's soft hands on my back, for games of catch with Joshua, for walks with Kalman, and for sausages sneaked to me under the table by Herschel.

If I didn't seize this opportunity, I would end up getting used to my new, foreign name. I wanted my real name back.

It is better to try and fail, I told myself, than to fail to try.

It was now or never. I leapt over the shrubs and turned toward one of the side alleys.

On the streets, they had started to light the street lamps. Darkness descended. Bloodthirsty teenagers appeared, faces half hidden in the dark. As I ran from shadow to shadow, I could see them beating, burning, and shattering windows. Scared, I found a hiding place in a dark alleyway. Dozens of boys gathered at the end of the street, piling books upon books. One sent a torch flying, and within moments, the pile rose into a ball of fire. The great light blinded me and I was struck by fear. Fire was the element I loathed most, and I was paralyzed by the thought of my fur being consumed by the flames.

Suddenly, I heard a familiar voice searching for me. "Zelig, Zelig . . . Zelig. . . ." Frank called loudly. I was surprised that he had not given up. I had to decide quickly what to do. One end of the alley was blocked by the book-burning boys. Frank's shadow was nearing at the other end. This is it, I thought. I am as good as caught. I was already imagining Frank dragging me back to his home and wife.

But he still hadn't noticed me and there remained in my heart a sliver of hope. The sun had set, and Frank would almost certainly not persist in his search much longer. Still in my hiding place behind the dumpster, I brought all my extremities as close to my chest as caninely possible, compacting myself as best as I could.

Frank was coming closer. "Zelig, Zelig. . . ." He was just feet away. I kept close to the ground, silent as I could be. Frank turned this way and that, surveying the scene one final time.

"Treacherous, ungrateful Jew dog," he said angrily, and headed home for dinner with his Greta.

I remained glued to the sidewalk behind the dumpster, wondering why I was chased by such misfortune. I thought once more of the hunt, the motionless kitten, Karl Gustav's triumphant barks, and worst of all, my unforgivable silence. At that moment, I took a vow: never again would I shed feline blood. Then I looked up at the horizon, at the roofs and the dark canvas of sky stretched between them. Was there someone up there to hear my vow?

Another doleful memory then arose. The image of my siblings, whom I would never see again. Woe is me, a house pet I had been, with the riches of my owners clutched between my paws; now they clutch nothing. I have no one to protect me, to feed me, to fill my water bowl. Where are Herschel's warm legs to press against on the cold, windy nights?

I rose slowly from my hiding place and walked onto the street. The scents that used to spark my curiosity now forewarned danger. Cars out to hit, police horses with hooves fit to kill, and worst of all – restless hoodlums, ready to throw any object in reach.

An arm came suddenly through the dark and grabbed at my throat. It caught my collar, and I heard Frank's voice growl at me. "Here you are, you elusive Jewish bastard! You thought you could escape! Ha!"

I tried to shrink away, preparing to receive the lashing an unruly dog deserves. But instead of a big *zetz*, I was surprised with a hug and a petting. Frank held my face between his hands. "All right," he said. "The doctor was right. I wasn't giving you the attention you need. Not to absolve myself of blame, but it's Greta's fault! Ach, what do you know? You just want to chase sticks with your friends. You don't need to grovel to a rich father-in-law and work hard to support a hellcat. Just as you live by the grace of my hand, I live by the grace of hers and her family's. If it weren't for her father, I wouldn't have enough money to fill a dog's dish. Dammit, Zelig, my life is in the dumps. Thank God I found myself a cute little idiot like you."

The next few days were divine. Frank and Greta shouted at each other more than usual, but it didn't impede my blessed walking routine. Every day, Frank would take me out for a long afternoon stroll. "I have to get to the office," Frank would tell Greta. He then left to visit Maximilian instead.

Every time we entered his home, Max would feed me a biscuit out of his hand, and then treat my belly to a nice rub. Just as he did well by me, he did well by Frank, and softly rubbed his belly as well. Frank would blush a little, peek at me – as though making sure his secret was safe with me – and succumb to Maximilian's petting.

CHAPTER 16

I had already learned from my limited life experience that loud, measured knocks meant trouble. Indeed, the deliberate knocks heard on Frank and Greta's door one morning came to seal another chapter of my life.

Three men dressed in black stood in the entrance. Thanks to my well-developed sense of hierarchy, I immediately identified the senior ranking member. He addressed Frank and asked, "Are you Herr Frank Heinz?"

"Yes sir."

"My name is Theodor Dürer, Standartenführer Theodor Dürer. I would like to ask you, do you know a man named Maximilian Loyt?"

Frank lowered his head and answered in a strangled voice, "No, sir."

Even I could tell he was lying.

"Are you sure you don't know a man by this name?"

"I am certain."

"I regret that you choose to defile the German language with such lies. You will have to come with us to the police station and explain how it is that you don't know him, and yet your pictures appear in the photo albums in his house."

Frank's face fell.

"Quite embarrassing photographs, if I may say so myself . . ." Standartenführer Theodor Dürer said cheerfully.

His two accompanying officers snickered through their mustaches.

Greta appeared from the washroom wearing a bathrobe, and asked what the inquiry was about.

"A personal matter," Frank said, trying to avoid embarrassment.

"Excellent," she said. "I love personal matters."

"Let me speculate, Madam, that your husband is no virtuoso in the bedroom."

Greta, who was usually quite quick to catch on, still required further explanation. The photographs presented to her did not leave much room for doubt. She nodded her head in agreement.

"I must admit, officer, that recently I've sensed something new about my husband."

"I believe a daughter of the German race deserves more than this flaccid worm. Your husband's tendencies, to be subtle, are not in line with the vision of the Reich. I fear your husband will have to come with us at this time. Perhaps several weeks of discipline at Sachsenhausen will make a man out of him."

"I stumbled," Frank said. "It's true, I stumbled. I'm not really like that. . . ." He gave Greta a pleading look. "Please forgive me. Please give me another chance. . . . Just one more chance, I won't let you down, I promise."

Standartenführer Theodor Dürer looked at Greta. Greta looked away from Frank.

"What is Herr Officer's opinion?" she asked.

An unpleasant odor arose from Greta. With time I would learn that it is called vengeance.

"They always promise, and then . . . like a dog returning to its vomit. Frau Heinz can trust me, it is just a matter of time."

Greta frowned. "Take him," she said dryly, and the odor intensified as she pointed at me. "And while you're at it, take away his Jew dog, too."

"Jew dog?" Theodor asked, with a compassionate look on his face. "How can you insult an impressive dog like this in such a way?"

"If you believe this dog is impressive, then be my guest. Here is his food dish and here is his leash."

Greta did not forget her manners. As we walked out to the street, the three officers, a handcuffed Frank, and I, she called after us. "I wish the officer a *guten Tag!* I wish you all a *guten Tag!*"

Theodor turned back and answered with a curt bow and a Nazi salute. *"Heil Hitler."*

CHAPTER 17

"And who is this?" Theodor's broad-shouldered wife asked as she came from the kitchen to greet him. She was drying her hands on a dish towel. Frau Dürer warmed the house with a pleasant smile. Her presence was fair and proper. She crouched by my side and looked into my eyes with obvious affection.

"How happy our little Georg will be!" she cried. "What a wonderful surprise awaits him!"

Standartenführer Theodor Dürer told her how he had come to meet me, and she kissed him on the cheek, indicating that he had brought home a welcome guest.

"Mm, you smell good," Theodor said, and returned her kiss.

"It's the dress," his wife explained. "I just got it back from the cleaner a few minutes ago."

Theodor took two steps back and looked his wife up and down. Then he said decisively, "The dress becomes you."

His wife curtsied and replied, "Thank you, thank you."

Two hours passed before I heard the tap-tap of shoes approaching the door. The doorknob turned, and in the entrance – knapsack on his back, hair smooth and blond, and a mischievous look in his eyes – stood Georg. He was all grace and youth. I barely gave his mother time for an official introduction before I leapt into his arms. May this be proof to all the skeptics out there: love at first sight does exist! Georg ruffled my fur and sent his mother a thankful look.

"You got me a dog?" Georg's eyes were aglow.

"Your father brought him for you," his mother said, holding her son's head between her hands. "And do you know why he brought you a dog? Because you are the cutest, sweetest child, and because the teachers at school have told us how good you are at gym and math."

"What's his name?" Georg asked his mother.

"Theodor," the mother called out, so her husband could hear her from his study, "what's the dog's name?"

Theodor joined his family in the foyer, scratching his head. "I have no idea. I forgot to ask. Well, Georg," he said to his son. "Do you like him?"

"Yes, but we don't know what to call him."

"We'll come up with our own name," Theodor suggested.

They all fell silent, thinking.

A memory arose that made my blood freeze in my veins. I could see the Gottliebs sitting in their living room as they first chose my name.

"I know!" Georg's face lit up. "Let's call him Wilhelm!"

"Wilhelm is an excellent name," said Frau Dürer encouragingly.

"Yes," the father piped in. "If the name befits an emperor, it is good enough for our dog. Welcome shall ye be, Herr Wilhelm, in our humble abode."

"Come, Wilhelm," Frau Dürer called me. She gave me a piece of bread dipped in gravy. I scarfed down the offering and leapt to thank her with a lick, dragging my hot, wet tongue over her face and lips. She broke out in deep laughter and wiped off her mouth.

"Ach, what intimacy!" her husband cried, and came a step closer to whisper in her ear without their son hearing. "All the flowers I had to buy for you, and for your mother, before I dared kiss you like that!"

"You could have kissed me from the very first day we met," she whispered back with a wink. "Too bad you didn't try."

I had no reason to escape from the Dürer's house. On the contrary, with each passing day, my memories faded and my time at the Gottliebs grew hazy. The only moment that reminded me of the Gottliebs was when Georg tried a new trick and placed me in front of the large mirror on the closet door. Although it was not a new experience for me, I pretended to be mesmerized. I had a feeling it would make him happy. Whenever I did remember my days with the Gottliebs, I couldn't help but feel disgusted by the odor of fear that accompanied those fleeting shadows of memory. I couldn't separate the memories of my puppy days from the pungent stench of fear. At the Dürers, however, fear was no longer in my vocabulary. Here, everyone was safe, their future was secure. There was nothing but optimism in the air.

Asher Kravitz

"Such an occasion cannot be ignored," Standartenführer Theodor Dürer said, his voice authoritative. "I've invited a special chef to prepare a three course meal for us."

"Oh, Theodor, you needn't have!"

"Wait until you see what's on the menu. French turtle soup. . . ."

"Ooh-la-la," his wife said, "that sounds expensive. . . ."

". . . roasted pig with gravy, and a Bavarian cream delicacy." The moment he pronounced the final word, there was a knock on their door.

The cook placed her masterpiece in the kitchen, took her fee, and disappeared. The officer and his wife clinked their glasses together and drank with their arms interlocked. She drank from his glass and he from hers.

Kalman and Shoshana had never laughed like that.

"And now I will request of my lovely wife, the new chairwoman of the SS Officer Wives Club, to show me the new apron she designed for the wives."

"To be honest, I'm a little disappointed with how it came out. The red isn't bright enough and the eagle is too small."

"I want to see the apron!"

Frau Dürer returned from the bedroom, with a red, black, and white apron tied to her waist. "You see what I mean? The red is a little pale, isn't it?"

Theodor rose and hugged his wife. He whispered in her ear. "I meant that I want to see you in nothing but the apron. . . ."

He looked at his wife in the same way I'd look at Shoshana Gottlieb after I stole a biscuit from the bowl on the table. Frau Dürer showed no resistance and he placed his hand at the back of her head and kissed her on the lips. She wrested

110

her arms out of his hug and stroked his shoulders. "I'm so proud of you," she said, "my Standartenführer." Theodor drew his wife toward the living room sofa.

"Oh, Hildegard," he said, his breath heavy. "I swear by the Fuhrer's mustache, you're just as beautiful today as you were the day we met at the rally."

"Wait a second," she tried to cool her eager husband. "The apron will get wrinkled."

The Standartenführer leaned his wife on the sofa, facing the big picture that hung on the wall. It was a strange portrait, set in a heavily ornamented frame. The face in the picture had a square mustache and glassy eyes that shone with a visionary glint. Something in his look reminded me of Spitz, the small and hot-tempered pinscher that would often bark at me in my younger days. The pinscher-man in the picture was raising one arm high in the air.

Theodor peeled off Hildegard's new apron and she threw herself into his arms. He held her tightly as he unbuttoned her shirt and hummed in her ear:

"My sexy wife will be my treat
because I am a dog in heat.
How much I like to touch with grace
a beauty of the superior race."

They were soon reenacting the intimate spectacle that Karl Gustav and his Rottweiler girlfriend had performed in the park.

"Look how he's watching, the little bastard," Theodor said when he noticed that I was staring at them, utterly hypnotized. But Frau Dürer would not be distracted. She hit the wall with the palm of her hand and moaned words that I wasn't familiar with. When they finished, they sat on the sofa and smoked. They were as exhausted as I would be after a long hour of tag.

"I'm as hungry as a bear that just awoke from hibernation," Theodor said, and extinguished his cigarette.

"Then let's go," Hildegard replied. "The table is set and the food is still warm."

Georg got home as his parents finished washing the dishes, drying them, and placing them back in the cabinet. Paul and Lars, Georg's good friends, were also over for the night. I discovered a new passion in my time spent with Georg and his friends – the passion for sticks. Nearly every time Georg's friends came over, we went out to the park across from the wide road. The vast lawns were welcoming, inviting us to play fetch endlessly. Georg would throw a stick as far as his little arms could manage, and I'd dart like an arrow to catch it and bring it back for another throw. Sometimes Lars would irritate me, pretending to throw the stick, but actually hiding it behind his back. I fell victim to this ploy more than once. But despite the insult in Lars's trickery, altogether I was very fond of Georg's friends.

Lars, who was always roller-skating, would often take me on walks, and Paul took me once to visit his father's shop. His father worked in a shop with a high ceiling, and huge hunks of meat hanging from hooks. Paul and his father collected a great number of quality pig bones for me.

Richard was Georg's best friend, but not mine. At first, Richard was very nice to me. He gave Georg much advice on how to best raise me, how to make me an obedient and disciplined dog, and how to turn me into a proper attack dog. He also helped Georg rid me of fleas and trim my nails. Richard had a strange odor, and I was quite sure that he had another dog in his life. I was not mistaken. Richard was the proud owner of Starky. I have no idea why I felt so hostile toward Starky. I think I was scared of him, but equally respected him. However, the thought of him placing a paw in my house was unthinkable.

When Richard attempted to call upon us with his dog, I barked, enraged, prepared to fight my last fight. Starky was a wolfish dog with a thick coat of fur and a wide skull. From the moment he set foot in my doorway, I was set to attack. I ran toward the door, barking as though I was possessed. Starky responded with barks of his own that resonated from the bottom of his lungs, indicating great power.

"Wilhelm, quiet! Quiet! Quiet, Wilhelm!" Frau Dürer tried to subdue my barking. "What's gotten into you? Who taught you to bark like that? What is this savagery?"

Her protest silenced me but for a brief moment. As soon as the door opened just a crack, I began barking again, and Starky pulled on his leash, barking at me twice as ferociously. We both bared our teeth and began snapping at the air. This was no game – my determined barks said it all – if this dog enters, blood will be spilled.

Hildegard held my collar and turned me away with her leg. "Maybe it would be better if you came over without Starky," she said through the crack in the door. "I don't think our dogs get along." I wouldn't back down and kept barking, so Frau Dürer called her son. "Come on, Georg, take your crazy canine."

Georg ran down from his room, and took me out for a lengthy walk. On the way, we met his classmate Beate and her father. "So, what's new at home?" Beate's father asked. Georg eagerly told Beate and her father about my exploits. He told them proudly of my might, and how I chased Starky away with my intimidating barks. "You should have seen Starky," he told them. "He almost died of fright. He was lucky my mother wouldn't open the door. Wilhelm would have torn him to pieces in seconds."

Over dinner, Frau Dürer told her husband about the day's events and mentioned my wild behavior when Richard came with his dog.

Theodor wasn't surprised. "Yes," he said. "Twice now on our morning walks with the dogs, Richard's father and I have met. It's clear the dogs aren't going to be the best of friends. I think there's a conflict between them over who's stronger and more dominant. Thankfully, while they're hardly sympathetic toward one another, they fear each other, and when they meet, they don't go beyond barking and flexing their muscles."

"I don't understand how these animals' minds work. How do you understand Wilhelm so much better than I do? Maybe it's because you men are so like dogs!"

Naturally, Frau Dürer was half joking, and she smiled at her husband.

"Do you really believe that?" her husband asked and came closer to her. He stood by her side and held her shoulders affectionately.

"At times," she replied.

"I think that in most ways, we are better than dogs, but in other ways, we have a great deal to learn from them."

"It wouldn't hurt men to learn a little loyalty from them. . . . I'm not talking about you, of course, but if we were to take your commandant, for example. . . ."

"If I may defend my kind, I'd like to point out that we do not defecate in the middle of the road!"

"Depends when. And besides, you men are even more bloodthirsty than dogs. You're always out looking for fights. Men don't just bark and flex their muscles. . . ."

They spoke on, but I, getting the whiff of a cat fight in the yard, went off to bark from the window. The cats turned to and fro looking for the source of the barking, and then went on their way. I looked at the world spread out before me. It was not my first time looking out a window this way, but this time everything looked different. This world was completely threat-free. Now this world was mine, bright, and without any obstacles. The Dürers didn't fear every government official that passed by. Soldiers didn't make them shiver, and even rowdy groups of misbehaving teenagers didn't scare them. Life without the burden of fear was infinitely nicer. I could breathe without that burning sensation, without suffocation. The air around the house had no stench of fear.

At nightfall, after Hildegard turned off all the lights and the two parents kissed their son goodnight, Georg invited me into his bed and spent an hour rubbing my belly.

"Can you keep a secret?" he asked me. "And even if they torture you, you won't tell anyone?" Then he hugged me, rested my head on his chest and petted my neck, and called me "Beate." He kissed me a few times until he fell asleep. Under the cover of night, his parents sneaked into our room. I opened a single eye, and they signaled that I should keep quiet and still. Theodor was holding some kind of strange box in one hand and a stick in the other. He turned the box toward us. There was a click, and a spark of light flew out of the stick. Georg's parents stood for a few more moments watching us, as the sight of their child, dreaming sweet dreams, hugging child's best friend, melted their hearts.

CHAPTER 18

*E*ven though I walked into the kitchen when they were already deep in the conversation, I distinctly remember what was said.

"Of course it'll be hard for me," Frau Dürer said, "but you simply cannot miss this opportunity. Theodor, I know this isn't a simple decision . . . and ultimately, it's your decision to make. But it's important to me that you know I'm one hundred percent behind you, and I think you should send them an affirmative answer. You know that many officers wait in line for years for such an offer to come their way."

"You don't know how difficult it is for me to leave you like this. . . . By the way, when do you plan on telling your parents?"

"I prefer to wait a while, perhaps at the beginning of my second trimester."

"They'll be angry when they discover that I left you in such a state."

"I'll tell them that I forced you," his wife said soothingly. "Besides, I'm sure you'll get a few days of leave in the spring."

"And what will you do with Wilhelm? It'll be hard for you to take him out. He's much stronger than he looks. Sometimes he tugs on the leash so hard that my shoulder practically comes out of its socket."

"You don't need to worry. . . . Truly, Theodor, I'm asking you, don't worry. I'm strong enough to take him out for his walks. And Georg will help too."

"Georg will be sad. . . ."

"Georg will understand that you're doing this for him, more than for anyone else. You see Georg as though he's still crawling around in his diapers. Georg is not a baby anymore. He's quite the little man."

Theodor fell silent and mulled over the matter.

"Think about it," his wife said. "Your salary will be doubled, and you'll be able to buy him whatever he wants. Besides, he'll be so proud. You know how his friends will look at him when he tells them that his father is the commander of the Waffen-SS cadet course. You'll make Georg a hero!"

One month later (I always followed the waxing and waning of the moon) the first letter came. Georg sat attentively as Frau Dürer read it to him.

"Dear Hildegard, Georg, and Wilhelm,"

Upon hearing my name, I joined the two, seating myself at Georg's feet and listening to every word.

"My first few days have been full of activities from dawn to dusk, and yet I found time to write to you. The previous commander of the camp, Herr Opitz, will be here next week as well, to continue training me. Without his help,

I'd probably be lost. We have excellent chefs here, so you needn't worry, I won't be tightening my belt. In less than two weeks the new cadets will arrive, and everything must be ready by then. I still haven't been paid my first salary, but as I understand, from the beginning of next month, I'll be receiving a salary, slips for laundry, clothing and shoes, and small change for cigarettes and newspapers. . . ."

At this point I lost interest and went searching for the source of an annoying buzzing sound emanating from the vicinity of the window. I had guessed correctly – a large fly was stuck in the space between the window and the screen. I tried to swipe at it with my paw, but the glass pane stood between me and the pleasure of squashing it.

I returned to the kitchen where Frau Dürer was reading the last lines of the letter. "When I get my new ranks, I'll send Georg my old ones. If he's taking good care of his mother, he deserves them more than I. And last but not least, I have a short message for our dear Wilhelm. Please read it to him. I'm sure he's smart enough to understand."

Hildegard followed her husband's instructions. She looked at me and read on.

"Wilhelm, you have an important job now too. You must not tug on the leash too fiercely, and help Georg take care of Mother. I know you're an exceptional dog, and I have the utmost trust in you!"

I was filled with a sense of pride that I had never known before. Frau Dürer looked back at her son and read the last line, "I miss you all very much, Theodor."

She wiped away a tear and stroked her son's head. "I'll write back to him, and leave you a few lines at the end to write your own message."

"And then can I go over to Lars's with Wilhelm?"

"After you write, you can go to Lars's, but please be back by nine, and don't forget to send my regards to his parents."

Hildegard applied a deep red lipstick and kissed the letter.

"Oh dear, it seems my lipstick is almost empty," she said. "Tomorrow I'll go buy a new one." She applied the rest of her lipstick to my paw and added my own signature to the letter.

"We can write 'Wilhelm's signature' next to it," Georg suggested.

"There's no need, darling." His mother smiled at him. "Father will understand."

The next day, after Georg left for school, Hildegard took the leash and hooked it to my collar. "Wilhelm," she said in a didactic tone, "now we're going to the post office to buy stamps and send Theodor the letter. I ask that you behave yourself, and please don't bark too loudly. It's hard for me to walk, and I have a slight headache." I trotted obediently by her side, enjoying the soft, refreshing drizzle. I swear, I tugged on my leash only once, and even then it was an accident. Head high, I strode at her heel, ignoring the food scraps on the ground, the opportunities to sniff, and the dogs passing by. I am on duty, my proud stride announced. I am protecting my lady and I have no time for trivialities.

Upon returning home from the post office, we were surprised to find two SS officers waiting by our front door.

"Frau Dürer?" they asked.

"Yes," she said distractedly, rummaging for the keys in her purse. "What is this about?"

One of them held a bouquet of flowers, the other an official envelope.

"Good morning, Frau Dürer," the holder of the envelope said in a low voice. "My name is Adolf Sturm and this is my adjutant, Fredrick Bachfeld. I was your husband's commander. May we please come in?"

"Did something happen?" she asked, her voice tightening. "Did something happen to Theodor?"

"I'm afraid your husband was hurt. He was driving a motorcycle last night. . . . . May we please come in?"

"Yes. Yes, of course."

The three sat on the couches and Adolf picked up from where he had left off. "I saw him turning toward the gate, he waved at me. A minute later, the alarm sounded and everyone settled in their machine gun positions. We were having a base-wide exercise. One of the new cadets wasn't careful, and he shot off a volley of bullets. One of the bullets hit your husband's leg and he overturned on his motorcycle. . . . He was killed on the spot. . . . He was a commander in his soul. Not just someone who orders others around. He believed in setting an example. He loved working with his soldiers. He was one of the most devoted officers I know. You have every reason in the world to be proud of him."

Hildegard gaped at the two officers, dumbstruck.

"We found this letter on his desk, I believe it's for you."

I could tell by the movements of her head – back and forth, up and down – that she read the letter several times.

Her gaze traveled here and there, as though she was lost inside her own house. Her entire body began to shake. She pulled her hair with her hands and a short moan of raw pain escaped her. Then she began weeping. "No," she mumbled through her tears. "This can't be happening."

"Frau Dürer," Adolf said, "I know that in moments like these, nothing can be of comfort. But I want you to know, and I mean every word that I say, you are not alone. The SS family and the entire German people are with you. You can come to me for anything you need, any time."

"This is the phone number for our office," the adjutant said, and placed a piece of paper on the table. "I'll be over again next week to see if there's any way I can help."

Hildegard stared at him and said nothing.

I sat down by her and laid my head on her lap.

"Why? Why?" she asked me. "Tell me, Wilhelm, why?"

The officers sitting on the other sofa exchanged glances without a word.

CHAPTER 19

*A*fter the officers' visit, Georg grew callous and distant. On the days that he went to school, he came home angry and grumbling. His mother tried to reach out to him, but he kept his answers curt and shut himself in his room. He would stay behind his closed door until his friends called him to join the youth movement activities. Only when he went with his friends to the youth movement did a spark of excitement appear in his eye. This spark grew when he'd unleash me on Gypsy children after the activities.

We went to the youth movement with Lars, Paul, and Richard. I enjoyed watching Georg marching with his friends. He was so graceful, swinging each arm and leg with perfect coordination. After the marching exercises, Georg and his friends would listen to their counselors.

"Who are we protecting ourselves from?" the counselor asked.

"From Jews and Bolsheviks," the well-trained Lars replied.

"And what does the Führer demand of us?"

"Obedience and sacrifice," Georg recited.

Later the boys would race and wrestle. The moments

when I had to watch one of the older boys bring Georg to his knees were as painful for me as they were for him. I jumped, barked, and lost control. Each time, I tried to go to my owner's aid, but the chain attached to my collar held me fast. I almost choked myself in my attempts to intervene and help Georg.

The best part of the youth movement was the hunting. At the end of each activity, the little Hitler Youths would depart in small groups to hunt Gypsies and Judes, singing a chorus of hate as loud as they could.

> *Bringt uns her einen Jud*
> *Auf dem Spiess ergeht ihm gut*
> *Und dann singen wir laut*
> *Haut den Schlangenkopf, haut!*

> Let's go find a dirty Kike.
> We'll impale him on a spike.
> Then together we will shout,
> hit the snake head. Knock it out!

Armed with bludgeons, Georg and his friends released their anger on each Jew that crossed their path. Men and women of every age and size were struck, with no discrimination. The excitement of the hunt awakened repressed instincts. A slumbering voice was stirred by the sound of trumpets. The pack would not rest until it smelled blood. With flashing eyes I released my anger as I chased the dirty Jews. The smell of their fear ignited my dark side. The cheers coming from Georg and his friends were fuel for the fires of hell flaming inside me.

But as I lay me down to sleep, I was revisited by the gloom of that day long ago, when I had hunted the black kitten with Karl Gustav and the tag club. The burden of regret was unbearable. One day, I entered Georg's room and found his closet door open. I examined myself in the mirror before me. There was a strange glimmer in my eye.

On one of the many nights of vagrancy, Georg and his friends recognized a young Jew. Although the street was dark and the Jew had his back to the pack, his hunched stride and curved back exposed his ethnicity.

"A Jew, Wilhelm!" Georg shouted, and I shot toward the boy at the end of the street with my usual determination, racing like a wild beast, ready to bite fiercely.

"Go on, Wilhelm! Go on, Wilhelm!" The cheers reached my ears.

Once again, I thought to myself, once again I can make my dear Georg happy. He'll hug me and tell everyone how proud he is of my performance.

The distance between me and the Jew was just four feet and it was time for the final pounce, but suddenly my ears pointed and my nose trembled with fear.

"Lay not thine jaws upon the child," a voice spoke, and goosebumps rose on my flesh.

"Lay not thine jaws upon the child and do not harm him!" My fur stood on end from tip to tail. I looked closely and the recognition struck me like lightning. The helpless Jew was none other than the child Moishe, Moishe, who was a guest at the Gottliebs' house for Seder night a lifetime ago.

"Get him, Wilhelm! Rip him up!"

"*Shema Yisrael!*" Moishe shouted a prayer, shielding his face with his hands.

I bit Moishe's shirt sleeve and tried to pull him away from Georg and his friends. Moishe didn't recognize me as his childhood friend, and in his distress, he hit my head.

"He's hitting Wilhelm," Richard shouted, and Georg and his friends ran toward us in order to exact revenge against the audacious Jew. I stood between Moishe and Georg. I growled as though possessed. Everyone looked at me, shocked into silence, as I walked in circles, barking and baring my teeth.

"What's wrong with him?"

"The Jude bewitched him!"

I ran like the devil had my tail.

Georg and his friends followed closely behind.

"Stop, Wilhelm, stop," Georg pleaded.

I looked back and noticed that Moishe had taken advantage of the fact that everyone was now chasing me, and he could escape from his pursuers.

Georg's calls didn't subside. He continued running after me even when all his friends gave up and stayed behind. Breathing heavily from effort, he continued shouting, "Stop, stop, Wilhelm . . . Wilhelm, please stop. . . ."

Georg's pleas tore at my heart. I couldn't listen to his broken voice any longer. I doubled my speed. My running was no longer the stumbling strides of a puppy. I ran like a powerful dog with well-formed muscles.

A new spirit uplifted me and I heard a loud noise from behind. As I ran, I shed my temporary names. **"Your name will no longer be Wilhelm, nor Zelig will it be,"** an ancient voice echoed in my ears. **"From now and forever, your name will be Caleb."**

126

CHAPTER 20

s my running wound down to a trot, I headed toward the Gottliebs' house. I wandered for hours. My paws became swollen from the prolonged walking, and the pads on the bottoms of my paws nearly wore through. The streets were covered in shards of glass. Pillars of smoke rose from every corner of the city. I took one wrong turn after another and followed paths that led me farther and farther from my birth home. Misleading voices had me walking astray; scents that seemed familiar led me off my path. And yet, each time I made a mistake, a higher power came along and set me straight on my way.

In a dark alley, I saw a group of young hooligans dressed in brown uniforms and armed with cudgels. They struck an elderly lady to the ground. One of them kicked her in the ribs, spat on her, and shouted, "You dirty, wrinkled Jewish whore." The boys stood over her and urinated. One of the boys saw me staring and threw a stone in my direction. The stone missed and I quickly retreated. The god of abandoned dogs was on my side.

At midnight I stood on my four exhausted legs in front

of my birth home. The curtains were drawn, and no light could be seen inside the house. I walked toward the entrance and climbed the familiar stairs. A dark fear of looming calamities snuck into my heart. I listened carefully and scratched at the door with my front paw. Not a sound was heard. Though I knew the house was uninhabited, I put my snout to the crack at the bottom of the door and tried to retrieve the trace of a scent. I couldn't smell anything but fresh paint. I barked, and immediately regretted doing so. I feared that angry neighbors would appear, to kick me away.

I waited for two more days, wandering the streets and gardens around the house. Those were my first two nights under the clear sky. On the third night, light emerged from the windows of the house. I saw that a new family had moved into the Gottliebs' home. I could feel goosebumps under my fur, and a sense of deep loss flooded my body. I would never see my dear family again. I realized I had become a stray.

*A broch iz mir!** I couldn't stand my own scent. I could feel how my body was overtaken by the stench of fear. The blood drained from my face. I had just about adopted that ever-terrified face – the face of a persecuted Jew. Days dragged on in an ominous routine. Some people would grant me half a sandwich, a biscuit, or a bone. Others would throw a rock, or even a kick in my direction.

* I'm in trouble!

I learned the hard way that humans were divided into the good, the bad, and the indifferent.

I spent most of my hours hiding under a bush or in the shaded corner of an alley. Sometimes, when the hunger and frustration became unbearable, I would follow people I saw in the street. "Look at that dog," a woman would say to her husband. "Look how he's following us. I think he's looking for a home."

Most people ignored me. At first, I tried to keep track of the time going by. One day, two days, three. Eventually I lost count, and my entire existence became an amorphous blend of wandering and survival. From courtyard to courtyard, dumpster to dumpster, and trash pile to trash pile. Another desperate attempt at a child's sandwich; once again following a lady with a pleasant scent of home, and then frustration once more. Sometimes I would linger near a passerby and he would bend down and pet me. These were brief moments of false hope.

One girl pointed at me as I passed her on the street, her face mirroring the look of wretchedness in my eyes. "Daddy, look what a cute doggy! Let's take him home."

Her father put a bit of sense in her head. "Leave him alone, he's just a dirty stray. When you grow up we'll buy you a real dog."

That wasn't the only instance. I can easily remember five different cases when merciful children called me to join them, but when we got home, their parents instructed them to send me away.

During the day I longed for the protection cast by darkness; at night I yearned for the warmth of day. Food, which I had always taken for granted as a pup, was now a rarity.

Each time I came across a makeshift meal, every time I was lucky enough to feel sated, the count began again: one day since my last meal, two days. . . . At night, the horrible sights I saw came back to me. The bonfires, the tall flames, charred pieces of paper detaching from books and fluttering away in the wind.

I walked the streets, avoiding stick-wielding boys and municipal workers. But it was the house dogs I worried about most. Those well-kept dogs who had owners, homes, and a lot of luck. Almost every day, no matter how well I concealed myself, I was sniffed out and chased away by the house dogs. Luckily, they were usually on a leash. After barking vehemently at me, they would turn their heads to their owners, waiting to be petted, as though they had served them well in chasing away an unwanted, despicable intruder.

Once I saw a little boy holding a pair of leashes, attached to a pair of large dogs. The dogs looked alike and seemed to be brothers. One of them noticed me and barked menacingly at me. His brother quickly tried to outbark him. The boy, surprised by his dogs' violent reactions, slipped and fell. The dogs, now free, began chasing me. They were well-fed, healthy dogs, and I was poor and hungry, a nothing, alone and abandoned. If it weren't for one brave lady who stood between us and waved her umbrella at them, their sharp teeth would have made me into a sieve.

I had no place in the world. I asked myself how much longer I could go on like this. I wondered when the fall would come from which there would be no rising. How would it happen? I asked myself. What should I expect? Dehydration, stupor, helplessly collapsing . . . and then the silent hope that it would end quickly. A relentless instinct forced me to be prudent. During the day, I made sure to stay in the shade. When I passed a puddle or a dripping tap, I drank all I could. I felt my energy slowly draining. I grew thinner and thinner each day, and it seemed that I would soon disappear. Little food found its way into my mouth during those weeks of wandering.

When the full moon was out, I would look at it, hypnotized.

The moon fascinated me with its magical bond.

One evening, I was walking by the Rosenpark, the park where I used to run and play tag with my friend Karl Gustav and the rest of the tag club. The park was empty, the benches deserted, and the grass bare. I walked through the park until my paws led me to the tree where the poor kitten had found his temporary refuge. I sat at the foot of the tree with my head held high and looked at the moon. The moon that governs the rise and fall of the ocean tides drew an age-old howl from my throat. My howl pierced the darkness and carried endless pain.

It was the way of the world – Esau hates Jacob, dogs hate cats. I tried to alleviate the heaviness of my heart but I was plagued by regret. The meow of that kitten was crying from the earth. If only I had stood between Karl Gustav and his friends and this innocent kitten. If only I had distracted them from the pointless hunt. If only I had chased away the boys. . . . But the truth gripped me: I could have saved the kitten and I had not.

I lay down by the tree and rested my face on the grass. Was this a worthy existence? I looked deep into my soul and asked myself, am I living a life worth living?

I closed my eyes, putting all the strength I had toward ignoring my hunger pangs, and fell asleep.

At midnight, a vision was revealed to me in a dream. Humanity had destroyed itself. Fauna and flora had gone with it into the nothingness, and I alone was left. The only creature to walk on four. A poetic and withdrawn dog, wandering among the ruins of a lost world. I was walking in a narrow canyon – an endless, winding dry riverbed. I could see the faces of my forefathers among the rocks. The clouds joined together to form the face of the Dog in the Sky. A huge Dog, dotted and spotted and colored by the clouds and sun.

The Heavenly Dog barked in a deep voice: **"Get thee out from thy country and from thy birthplace."**

CHAPTER 21

I heeded the command of the Heavenly Dog and left the city. I wandered the suburbs and sent barks out every which way. Between barks, I would pause and listen. I waited to hear if other dogs were barking as well, searching, like me, for more of their kind. I could hear a distant echo of barks coming from the orchards that filled the valley. I walked toward the sounds. There was no need to teach me this valuable lesson; I knew very well that "alone" meant "dead." In the company of other dogs, I would be able to hunt better, and I would be protected. We dogs are so worthless as individuals, yet so majestic as a pack.

In one of the peach orchards in the southern suburbs, I met a pack of stray dogs.

One of the dogs, a mixed mastiff who was almost the size of a wild boar, walked toward me slowly, his paces even. He stood near me, just a bite away, frozen like a statue and looking straight into my eyes. I looked back at him with reverence and awe. He raised his tail, exposing his privates to show how fearless and self-assured he was. Here's a fierce dog, I thought. Only a complete fool would disrespect him.

He barked twice – *I am the leader*. His ears were pointy, his fur dense, his jaws frightful, and his barks rumbling. I leaned on my side in a submissive pose, declaring that I accepted his leadership.

He seemed satisfied. He walked away from me and rubbed against a female pack member, whom I'd later name Josephine. The message was clear: I was welcome as a member of the pack, but I should not dare to sniff his favorite cocker spaniel. Josephine was his, and she was off limits to the rest of the pack. I accepted the terms and joined in.

Altogether, there were seven members. Five males and two females. Three of the males were black border terriers. Although practically indistinguishable visually, their personalities could not have been more different. One, athletic with curly black fur, was an avid hunter and calculating to the bone. The second, also athletic with curly black fur, had a reliable character and tended to remain silent. The third, athletic with curly black fur as well, was reckless and fearless.

I was suddenly struck by an odd feeling: I felt the need to treat the members of the pack as humans did. I had difficulty acclimating to their presence without giving them, or at least some of them, names. I gave the border terriers names according to their traits: "Calculating," "Reliable," and "Reckless." It was clear from their habits that they had never lived with humans.

I named the leader of the pack Gonzales, and his mate Josephine, as I mentioned. Josephine didn't interest me. She had a fawning look and her bark was squeaky. I had my eye on the other female, whom I called Margo. I named her for one of the most beautiful puppies I had played with in my youth. Margo was a boxer with a firm backside. She was covered in short, tortoiseshell fur. She was my kind of bitch. We had only known each other for twenty seconds, and her head was already under my tail. My heartbeat quickened. Ach, blessed self-indulgence!

I watched her, bewitched, as she stretched, and the morning sun left gleaming lines on her fur. I am no great aesthete, but I swear, I've never seen anything finer than her in all of creation. Margo was a wanderer, and she had the same smell that Georg and his friends seemed to hate so much – the Gypsy scent. Just like her Gypsy family, Margo smelled of sweat and liquor. I suddenly felt sorry for all the times I had chased Gypsies, egged on by Georg and his friends.

Perhaps inspired by the mystical traditions of her previous owners, Margo enjoyed putting her snout to my leg and sniffing my paws at length. She examined them closely, as though she could find secrets in their lines.

On the very first day we met, she hinted with a rousing howl that I was welcome to jump her as I desired. It made me uncomfortable. Despite the ways of my kind, I had a modicum of shyness and modesty. I lowered my ears to show my embarrassment. *Your intensive courting*, I was saying, *is not quite to my taste, little virgin Jewish dog that I am.*

I eventually gathered my courage and approached her. I rubbed my snout against her neck, a delicate motion that, if translated into human tongue, would mean *Margo, my love, I would set my tail on fire for you!* But Margo wasn't satisfied with romantic gestures. She wasn't willing to forgo the throes of passion. She fluttered her pretty eyelashes and pulled me aside. . . . Margo, oh Margo, you were as fresh as a spring day when you rose from a dip in the river, shaking the water out of your fur at one hundred revolutions per minute. How I loved running with you at dusk through the wheat fields, biting at your heels, and charging at you with the lust of youth.

When I walked with Margo one morning to dip in the river, I glanced at my reflection in the water. I barely recognized the face that looked back. I was no longer the puppy that Reizel had placed in front of a mirror to watch his reactions, nor was I the same complacent dog who had looked back from the mirror set in Georg's closet door. A strong, muscular dog was looking up at me now. There was something of my mother's might in the image. My body was molded and designed to fit its purpose. The months of wandering, the hunger, the cold, and the hunt had made me stronger than ever.

The seasons came and went, bringing with them heat and snow. One evening, I heard strange whistles coming from the sky. I looked up and saw a flock of huge birds flying above in an organized formation. Large blocks were released from the underbellies of these birds like oversized droppings. I heard explosions, and pillars of smoke rose from the nearest city.

That evening, the border terrier Calculating got a thorn stuck between his teeth. The infection spread through his mouth and he grew weak. We saved pieces of rabbit from the hunt for him, but eating merely caused him more agony.

Each bite was followed by a yelp of pain. He lived on water for several more days until one morning, he got up and walked away from the pack. It was clear that we must leave him alone. He walked to and fro until he found shelter in the shade of a tree and collapsed. The fleas and ticks didn't wait until he met his maker. Having lost the ability to ward them off, they came swarming by the dozens. He gazed at the world with a glazed look as his last canine thoughts dimmed in his mind.

About a month after Calculating left the pack, we were joined by a thin, tall dog with huge ears. I named him Donkey Ears. He was a curious sort, excited by his mere existence, and he had a goofy smile permanently fixed to his face. Donkey Ears enjoyed following ladybugs and worms that crawled out of the bushes, but his chief obsession was chasing butterflies. Every time a butterfly flew over his head, he would leap and try to snatch it between his jaws. Being as clumsy and gangly as he was, he never succeeded in his mission. His incessant skipping pointed to his deep infantile state, and yet he was one of those creatures that it's hard to recall without smiling. I used to watch the butterflies flit away from his empty jaws and wonder about the secret of their flight.

As time passed, I rose in the hierarchy of the pack. The courage and loyalty I displayed proved their worth, and I was promoted to Gonzales's deputy-friend-confidant. Everyone obeyed me, and a bark from me was as respected as a bark from Gonzales.

Only the king shepherd, whom I called Lucas, refused to recognize me as deputy to the pack leader. Lucas's muscles were as densely packed as an army duffle; he had a scar on his snout and a black patch surrounded his mouth like a beard. He would raise a nonchalant ear at the sound of my barks, and would always challenge me by urinating in the places that I had marked. I made it clear that his behavior was unacceptable, but he ignored my angry barks. Once I even saw him urinate on an old urine stain made by Gonzales. That dog simply had no boundaries. From my very first day in the pack, I noticed that Lucas's admiration of Gonzales as the alpha male was fake and ingratiating. He would always pretend that he revered Gonzales, but there was scorn hiding beyond his impressed gaze, and conspiracy lurking behind his sycophantic eyes.

One day, I noticed that Gonzales seemed distressed. I guessed that his relationship with Josephine was in crisis. I also noticed that she was acting quite coldly toward our leader. I suspected that Lucas had something to do with it. That sneaking king shepherd had secretly conspired with Josephine. I had seen Lucas mocking Gonzales behind his back. When Lucas was around Josephine, he openly showed his aspirations for the crown, and she never even batted an eyelash! In fact, she displayed a cheerfulness that simply encouraged him. Shameless bitch!

Lucas feared Gonzales, but he wasn't scared of me at all, and so he would try to undermine my position among the pack with all sorts of provocations. Every time he'd bathe in the lake, Lucas made sure to get me wet with the water he shook off himself. He would also bark at ungodly hours, and then pretend he had woken me accidentally.

Once I woke up early in the morning with a stomachache. I chewed on some grass to try to subdue the pain. Suddenly I felt an urgent need to fill my lungs with as much air as possible. Something was shifting and trembling inside me. I was no longer the master of my own body. In order not to choke, I opened my mouth and raised my stomach. My eyes were wide open and choking sounds escaped my mouth. I puked. Raising my head, whom did I see but Lucas, watching me with scorn. He knew I wasn't fit to fight back, and he chased me away with a salvo of barks. I retreated and watched him helplessly as he ate my vomit.

On a different occasion, I was burrowing in the ground and came across a hearty bone. Lucas, stricken by jealousy, came running toward me and caught the other end of the bone in his teeth. I tried to shake him off but failed. He had a strong grip. In angry growls, I reminded Lucas of the rules of food: he who finds the food gets the food. The finder has the right to protect his find from any aggressor. I made it clear that I would not give in, and he had better let go because I'd bite him until he bled. Lucas barked back in defiance.

Gonzales, who was passing by, intervened without delay. He approached Lucas threateningly, and the latter immediately let go of the bone and retreated. Gonzales took the bone for himself as a trial fee, but I was satisfied.

I remembered Kugel and the stolen sock. I had just been recompensed.

Finally, justice had been served!

One morning, I woke up later than the rest of the pack and stretched lazily. Margo was digging in the ground. She extracted a juicy steak that she had hidden there a few days earlier, and came to eat with me. Gonzales had gone out with Donkey Ears and the two border terriers to hunt rabbits. An hour later, they returned short of breath, tongues wagging. They hadn't found any rabbits, but they had come across a fox and had run him into the ground. Gonzales had managed to sink his teeth in the fox's neck and the four enjoyed an excellent meal.

Three days passed, and then things took a turn for the worse. The first victim was Donkey Ears. His magnificent ears drooped and his eyes turned a sickly red. He collapsed onto his stomach and all his limbs quivered. It was clear that he would never stand up again. Soon Reckless and Reliable, the remaining border terriers, began drooling uncontrollably and shooting crazy looks in all directions. They smelled like death. In less than two days, they passed on from this world in seizures and coughs.

Finally, it was the hour of truth for Gonzales.

He began growling, his back arched and his tail tucked in. He barked at branches for no reason, and lunged at me and at Margo. We ran away from him, terrified. He would relax briefly, with a thoughtful expression, in the shade of the trees. When I watched him lying so calmly, a small hope crept into my heart that perhaps the threat of death had passed, but I could see the end glimmering in his dilated pupils. The illness raged and its effects were palpable. Gonzales's ears bent back, the hair on his neck stood on end, his stomach shrunk, and his ribs stuck out.

He rose from his resting spot and began chasing me, frenzied. There was barely a stride between us. I could practically hear the beating of his heart and the chattering of his teeth. Suddenly he froze in his spot. He was terror-stricken by a nearby trickling river. Who knows what visions of sulphurous and tormenting flames he saw in the stream? He fought the sickness for two more days and then let go. He lay motionless and waited. I approached him carefully, though I knew that he no longer had the strength to bite. Gonzales, who was now more bone than muscle, lifted his head as though he was asking for one more hour of grace. A loud bark escaped his mouth and pierced the air. It was his last. His jaws trembled and all that remained in his lungs was the shadow of a whimper. I tried to butt my nose into his snout just one last time, but our pack leader's head fell as he choked and died.

The memories began flashing before my eyes. I could see us running toward each other in a friendly brawl. At the end of our scuffles, I usually ended up on my back with Gonzales huffing and puffing above me, proud of his unbeatable strength. The powerful Gonzales with the fiery eyes, who needed just one look to petrify the entire pack. I closed my eyes and bowed my head. That mighty dog was now motionless at my feet. I sniffed around silently but the moment of mourning did not last long. Lucas began barking proudly, "The king is dead, long live the king shepherd." He galloped around the pack and, in loud barks, declared himself the new leader. Josephine barked along, accepting this new leadership.

Lucas looked straight at me now, a challenge in his eyes,

and his bark held the hint of a viper's hiss. "Gonzales is gone and you lost your protector. Let's see if you dare bite me now!"

"You bastard, you mongrel," I barked back. "Gonzales's body is still warm."

Lucas bared his teeth, and his psychotic barks sent a clear message: *you can't escape my powerful jaws.*

Am I a cur, I thought angrily, that he allows himself to bark at me like that? This is it, I decided. Time for action! Disgust at Lucas's greedy appetite and gluttonous eyes spread through me. He was stronger than I, his muscles better developed, but I got my strength from being the underdog. The key to victory is initiative! I charged with bared teeth, and sunk my fangs into the soft and vulnerable part of his neck that was covered in thick, curly hair.

It was a shame Greta couldn't see me now, I thought to myself. I would like to hear her call me a cowardly Jew dog now. Lucas was not quick to surrender. He caught my right leg in his mouth and flipped me forcefully onto my back. He wasn't going to let me recover from the fall, and stood above me. He caught the back of my neck between his teeth. The fight reached its deciding moment. If the king shepherd were to shake my head with enough force, my neck would break and I would find my death in the same way the black kitten in Karl Gustav's mouth found his. I took advantage of the only weakness that was within reach – his large ears. I tore through his right ear with my teeth. I could feel my fangs meet through his flesh. As Lucas howled in pain, I removed my neck from between his jaws and sunk my teeth back into his injured neck. I shook him with force, overtaken by the fervor of the fight, until his sight became blurred and he whimpered for his life.

I couldn't kill him.

I let go of the wounded dog and allowed him to stand on his four feet. Lucas rose. His tail remained fixed to his belly, his arrogant barks stuck in his mouth. I gave two last warning barks, and he bolted. Josephine, whose treason had been brought out into the open, disappeared as well, never to be seen again.

I shook the remnants of his bitter fur out of my mouth. Lucas's gloomy shadow was gone, but I was a leader without a pack. Just as I rose to the throne, I became an ex-leader. Five were dead, two had fled, and we two – Margo and I – were alone. We knew that if we remained in this province without a strong, united pack, we would soon meet our demise. We walked toward one of the village markets and scanned the area for snatches of food. Our plunder was meager. The crusts of a sandwich, some egg shells, and the skeleton of a fish that had already been picked clean by the village cats. Margo spotted a fat rat at a street corner and began to bark. It was a fat, old rat with a stump instead of a tail. It whistled in fear and began running back and forth, searching for refuge from us. Our hunger was distressing, and the option of eating the rat, being as much meat as any other option we had, was almost tempting. Margo approached the rat and sniffed it.

"Let it go," her look said. "Let the miserable creature go. It already smells like a carcass."

My desire to bite the rat subsided. I curled up with Margo on a newspaper, in a mutual attempt to enjoy each other's heat. Margo fell asleep in the blink of an eye, but I remained awake. I turned around and got up again and sat down again, trying hopelessly to improve my sleeping position. The street was completely silent. I understood that another chapter of my life had just come to a close. A strange scent of dissipated smoke was in the air. Memories of the huge fires that had chased me away from the city came drifting back.

My stomach ached so much from hunger, I thought I would wobble like a drunk and fall flat on my face if I'd try to stand straight. Within the whirlwind of unfocused thoughts rose the memory of terrifying sights. I remembered the fires from which I had run. I remembered the charred pages, the torn pieces of paper that had flown out of books and disappeared in the wind.

I was suddenly scared. I thought I heard voices speaking in my ear. Was I hearing the ticks talk? It seemed as though I could understand their language. They wouldn't stop praising the sweetness of my blood. Was I going crazy? I could swear that I heard the ticks cheering as they feasted.

Hush, bloody ticks! My body ached and I itched all over. The ticks laughed at me and drank on. The fact that I was scratching didn't interfere with their enjoying my warm blood. I tried over and over to get them off me, but it seemed that my helplessness was simply encouraging them.

Margo awoke from my rhythmic scratching.

"Is something bothering you?" her eyes asked.

I looked at her in desperation. "These ticks," I wanted to tell her. "I think I'm going crazy."

For a moment, I could almost hear her speaking in human tongue. Really? Could it be? I looked at her, but she didn't respond. She was deep asleep again. I couldn't understand – how could I be talking with her while she was sleeping?

If only we could speak in human tongue, I thought, what would I tell her?

I closed my eyes and felt Margo's paw resting on my forehead.

Love cures me and gives me strength, I would tell her. I wondered if that would impress her. *Every time I look at the moon*, I would add, confessing to her, *I can sense a greater power that draws a sad howl from the depths of my heart.*

The clouds parted and displayed the moon in all its paleness. Margo, who may not have been asleep at all, turned her ear toward me, asking to hear more. I sat up straight, patted the ground with my front paws and howled, directly into the heart of the moon.

Early the next morning, before the shops opened, two men dressed in black approached the newspaper on which we had spent the night. One of them threw a juicy, fragrant sausage onto the ground. Margo cowered from fright. She took several steps back. I was so hungry that I simply ignored her warnings: "Don't, my friend, don't be hasty."

The pangs of hunger in my stomach, which had shrunk so its walls could almost touch, had driven me out of my wits. The temptation was too great, and I didn't hesitate. I blocked out Margo's warning and began chewing. The excitement over this free meal was so great that it blinded my other senses and I didn't notice the odd aftertaste.

And behold, the sun was setting, and a heavy darkness came over me, and a fainting lethargy slackened my limbs.

"Caleb, Caleb, where art thou?"

The Heavenly Dog appeared to me in a blazing torch and a smoking furnace.

"I am here," I barked, "I am here!"

"What seest thou, Caleb?"

"I see a seething pot, filled to the brim with flesh."

"Not a pot," the Heavenly Dog corrected, **"but a furnace. To this furnace your people will come, those you love and cherish, and they will be enslaved and tormented for many days. And I will judge the nation who will torment and kill and burn and suffocate and behead and hack and slash and gash. You, however, will go to your ancestors in peace and be buried at a ripe old age."**

More was hidden than revealed. The Heavenly Dog was speaking to me in riddles. "Explain yourself," I tried to say, but though my jaws were moving, no voice was heard.

CHAPTER 22

I awoke with a terrible headache. I looked around.

Where was Margo? I leapt to my feet and barked like a mad dog, a great and mournful bark.

Margo was gone.

I am in a cage! I am caged and Margo is not with me.

It was hard to stand up straight. I was still dizzy and my legs were failing me. I tripped over the rusty bars of the cage. *I am in a trap, that's what a cage is. A cage is the worst of all fates.* I barked on and on as I tried to stand. I barked until my lungs ached and I collapsed, drained. *Where is Margo? Was she captured too? What would a dejected dog like her do, left all alone in the world?*

Although my senses were still blurred, I stood and stuck my snout in a space between two of the bars. Even a pinscher wouldn't be able to pass through these corroded bars – *indeed, I am caged. Trapped. A tiny, filthy cage, three strides wide and four strides long.* I paced from wall to wall like a captive lion. I looked around, examining my new surroundings. There wasn't much to learn. My cage was one of a long row, well-arranged as in a large prison. The noise was deafening. There were hundreds of dogs as unlucky as me, barking all around me.

I was surrounded by steel bars . . . and then suddenly, from within the snare, I had an epiphany. I remembered my dream and the Heavenly Dog. I felt as though something within me had changed – but what?

My sight had become more focused, but that wasn't the only change. My awareness was heightened.

I ceased thinking of myself and started thinking about Margo. There was a prayer in my heart, and I now knew to whom I must direct it. *O Heavenly Dog, please keep my Margo safe!* The fact that I would never see her again was crystal clear, casting a cruel and sobering light on the world. Lines of light and shadow striped my fur. I looked around again – what on earth was this place?

I closed my eyes and prayed for another stupor to descend.

A deep inner voice whispered that I must renew my strength, but I had no idea what for.

Closing my eyes didn't help. I knew very well that when I opened them, Margo would not be by my side. The cold concrete I was lying upon dashed my hopes that this was all just a bad dream. I eventually curled up in resignation next to my empty food dish. *This is my fate. So it has been decreed and so it will be.* I immersed myself in thoughts. I could now see the story of my life laid down on the axis of time. I wondered how many dogs were able to do that. Here is my history unfolded: I was born on a padded carpet, surrounded by petting and happiness. If it were up to me, I would have stayed in Kalman and Shoshana's house forever. I had learned the hard way that my fate was not determined by my wishes. I began feeling a little queasy. Much time had passed since I last thought about my puppy days. From there I had traveled, by German decree, to Frank and Greta. I tried to remember one moment of joy in that house, but came up blank. My attempts to escape had failed. After that, I moved to the Dürer house, with sweet Georg who treated me so well. . . .

A certain tension spread through all the cages and cut my reminiscing short. All the dogs in the pound stood up at once, barking loudly. The reason was soon clear – chow time. A fat man wearing a stained white apron came in, pushing a cart with a large cask filled with a fragrant mixture of rice, grain, and small strips of meat. He ladled servings into the food dishes of my fellow inmates. All my deep thoughts about my fate made way for more basic urges – I would finally have food in my dish – and, oh, how hungry I was!

A large female with a foxy face and a pointy snout was sitting in the cage across from me. She seemed defeated. Even when her dish was filled with a serving of the concoction, she approached it suspiciously, sniffed it, and went back to sitting in the corner. The cage on my left was inhabited by a thin dog with a long tongue. He seemed upset with his living conditions. There was an arrogant look in his eyes, and his wrinkled nose made it plain that this food was not up to his standards.

The food server reached my cage. He had a wide smile and fleshy lips. He looked like the kind of man in whose company his fellow humans weren't interested, and who therefore spoke most often with us quadrupeds.

"Ah, you've woken up, good morning!" he greeted me

cheerfully. "You were drugged too, hmm? Those National Socialists know what they're doing. Come, let me pet you, I'll give you a nice serving. I'll put lots of food in your dish. Stand up, eat, you have to be strong. Soon Doktor Plachtner will be here, and you don't want Herr Doktor to think you're a worthless wimp."

I gorged myself on the food as the chatty fat man watched me. Then I drank from the bucket in the corner of my cage.

"Aha," he said, when he saw how I was licking the bottom of my dish clean. "You have quite the appetite. You must still be hungry. Maybe I'll give you some more."

My eyes told him that I thought that was an excellent idea.

"Okay, come here, I'll give you an extra serving."

Before I started on my second serving, I thanked him with a lick.

"You're a nice dog," he said, petting me generously. "All the other dogs run straight for the food and pretend that I don't exist. Take good care of yourself, you! When Herr Doktor comes, be very alert. The Selection Doktor is as important as God – he determines your fate! Listen closely, doggy," he said, furrowing his eyebrows. "When Herr Doktor looks at you, don't look down. Look him straight in the eye. Growl like you're the surliest dog in the pound. Herr Doktor likes them strong and bloodthirsty. You don't know this, but this here is merely a transit station. The strong and lucky ones will be taken through professional training and will be placed in our security forces. The weak ones will be taken to hospitals to help medical students practice their surgical skills. . . ."

His concern was touching. I guessed by his look that he

didn't suspect I could understand what he was saying. If I were in his shoes, I wouldn't suspect anything either. How could he know that the apparition of the Heavenly Dog had bestowed me with wisdom?

When I finished eating my second serving, I continued surveying my new surroundings. Despite the numerous transitions in my life, this time it was harder than ever to acclimate. The pangs of hunger had subsided, but it was hard for me to exchange the wide open green plains for this small cage which couldn't even fit a Seder table.

The man pushing the cart paused by one of my neighbors. The neighbor was a ginger dog with white eyes. When the man dished his food out, he called the dog by name. "Ah, Pierre-Toulouse, how are you this morning?"

Pierre-Toulouse replied with gruff barks. I peeked at him – something in his barks seemed unconvincing. He smelled like one who had been spoiled in his youth, but he barked like a fighter. It was clear, however, that his barking greatly impressed some of the dogs around him.

Next I set my gaze upon a small dog with reddish eyes. Her belly was swollen and she smelled of gestation. She lay there as one who accepted her fate.

Footsteps could be heard approaching from the path that crossed the pound. It was the Doktor, walking through and examining my fellow prisoners. The Doktor had two assistants, and both wore white coats. They each held a binder and obediently wrote down everything he said. The three walked from cage to cage. When the Doktor was welcomed by a ferocious canine outburst, he motioned with his right hand. If he was welcomed indifferently or with a wagging tail, he motioned with his left.

Doktor Plachtner and his escorts reached my cage for my moment of truth.

"And how about you, my friend?" the Doktor asked as he clanged on my cage bars with his pencil. My response was a great assault, bloodcurdling growls, and blazing looks that demonstrated my aggressive qualities.

"When this one bares his fangs," the Doktor said to his escorts, with just a dash of humor, "it is terrifying enough to stop England and Russia in their tracks!"

The escorts smiled as was their duty. It seemed the three had fallen for my charade. The Doktor motioned with his right.

After my cage, they went to Pierre-Toulouse's cage. He who had barked so loudly before received them submissively. He walked meekly toward the Doktor, showing his readiness to accept the Doktor's mastery.

The Doktor came by the next day and lifted Pierre-Toulouse by the scruff of his neck. I felt sorry for him. His sad look broke my heart. Pierre-Toulouse was shaking all over as he looked at the Doktor with droopy ears and his tail between his legs. Pierre-Toulouse was placed in a large cart along with the rest of the weaklings and cowards.

The devil does not buy a soul without a body.

We were loaded – canines in cages – onto a truck, and set off on our way. As long as the truck kept to paved roads, everything was fine. On the dirt trails, we got bumped and bruised all over. It was hard to steady ourselves against the rocking truck, yet the trip was interesting. We passed many rivers and creeks. Women were out washing clothes and fishermen waited patiently for their lunches. The world slowly turned dark. The sun began to set and the shadows stretched until they disappeared. The very last beams of light shone on the fences of the Central Training Facility for Guard and Assault Dogs.

A tall man with a rifle stood sentry at the large iron gate. He asked the truck driver for his documentation and took down the details. We were let into the facility, and each dog was placed in a large, spacious cell. There was a doghouse in the corner of each cell, and food and water dishes stood at each entrance. These Germans were such an orderly nation. It was simply a pleasure.

Each of us was given a name and a trainer. My new name was Blitz. My fourth name in less than six years. My personal trainer was a thin, tall, and sympathetic man named Ralph Schmidt. Ralph had a long, pointy noise and big ears. He reminded me a little of Donkey Ears, may his soul rest in peace. He had the same clumsy gait. His movements also reminded me of the wobbly *lulav* that Kalman used to carry on *Sukkos*. His uniform was so big on him that it seemed as though it could fit two Ralphs.

My relationship with Ralph began in a bucket. He filled a bucket halfway with water, poured some disinfectant inside, placed me in, and began to scrub. The water was a little too hot for me and Ralph's tickling motions made me uncomfortable, but I was scrubbed clean. Dozens of ticks and fleas that had made my fur their home began floating in the soapy water, twitching and jerking.

"What have you done, you cursed cur!" one of the ticks shouted at me. I recognized its voice; it was one of the ticks that had been laughing at me just a few days prior.

"I have decided to keep my blood to myself," I barked. "I'm afraid you'll have to make do with the soap water!"

"Ah yes, Blitz," said my devoted trainer. "You do like taking baths, very good. We'll get all this dirt off you and make you into a dazzling dog. What an improvement already! A moment ago you were just grey, and now your fur is clean – the white is white and the black is black."

After he washed me a second time in clear water and rinsed out all the soap, he began brushing me. With each brush stroke, he tore out all the knotted hair that had formed around the thorns that were caught in my fur.

Ralph took care of everything I needed. Every day he took me out for three walks, and twice a day he'd fill my dish with excellent meat. We would walk without a leash. He would throw pinecones and I would bolt like an arrow to bring them back. In order to improve our physical fitness, they would let us dogs out every evening. We would run around, playing together until we ran out of steam.

Our routine included two training periods each day. The morning was focused on the art of order and discipline. The afternoon was devoted to defense and assault. In the mornings, we learned how to walk on our trainer's left side, how to sit, lie, and stay still until told otherwise. We also learned how to run along a marked line and pass between empty barrels. In the afternoons, we practiced barking at the signal of a hand, baring our teeth on command, chasing an escaped convict as a team, and charging at a cloth scarecrow. A successful attack, one that ended with teeth in the neck or a bite at the groin, received a round of applause from the trainers.

During the training, I noticed what poor concentration skills my fellow canines had. After twenty minutes of training, they would look bleary-eyed at their trainers, as though their brains were on the brink of collapse. Not to brag, and in all honesty, twenty minutes of training were a piece of cake for me. I remembered that in my puppyhood, I often asked myself if dogs and men were one and the same. Now it was clear to me that they were different species, but I still wondered which one I was closer to.

The morning training was held in groups, and the evening training was one-on-one. In the mornings we stood together, each dog with his trainer, in front of a wooden platform upon which stood the head trainer, Jorgen Klein, accompanied by his dog Schwantz. Schwantz was an example of intelligence and obedience to us all.

"*Sitz!*" Jorgen Klein commanded, standing by his dog and pointing his finger down. Schwantz would sit, straight-backed and regal, aware of his perfect performance. After the demonstration, each trainer would turn to his trainee. Ralph knew I had no need for this training. He'd just whisper "*sitz*" and I would be in sitting position immediately. Out of respect to the head trainer, Ralph never complained about the wasted time. Every morning, I would carefully carry out each order Ralph gave me, much to the pleasure of the men in charge. In the evenings, I would work with Ralph on much more complex procedures. He would hide metal plates underground, and I would mark their locations by sitting next to them and barking. At the clap of his hands, I would jump over a fence. Two claps and I would crawl underneath. Ralph would lie on the ground, feigning injury, and I would catch his coat collar between my teeth and drag him to safety. I completed our final exercise flawlessly – I swam across a deep puddle, carrying a baton in my mouth.

One evening, we were all called into the briefing room. My friends and I sniffed each other calmly. Jorgen Klein's entrance into the room was accompanied by a loud *"Achtung!"* and the room fell silent. Klein cleared his throat, looked straight at us, and said, "I have already mentioned that you will be joining real military activity before you finish this course. This will be an important test for you and for the dogs you will be working with. Indeed, this moment has arrived. Allow me to present the commander of the central sector of the Generalgouvernement, Obersturmbannführer Klaus Mitternacht."

CHAPTER 23

We sat, each dog and his trainer, in the back of a truck that headed east. The drive was bumpy and long, and the need to urinate was getting harder to control. The floor of the truck was metallic and uncomfortable. The heavy mechanical sound that accompanied the ride didn't make conversation easy.

"I've actually heard that Lublin is a very nice city," the man seated next to Ralph said loudly.

"The Old Town is quite nice," Ralph confirmed. "But we're not going to be walking around that area today."

When they finally let us off the truck, we found ourselves in an area of densely crowded, demolished houses. The sidewalks were broken, and a trail of fetid waste ran along the side. I hurried to find a proper wall to answer the call of nature. My fellow dogs and their trainers followed my lead. One of the dogs urinated very near the wall I had found. I barked at him, uncomfortable. I hate it when they urinate too close to me.

After a few moments of stretching and familiarizing ourselves with the area, Ralph commanded, "Blitz, come!"

He separated me from the rest of the dogs and trainers in order to keep me away from any scents that might distract me. He brought several shirts and pairs of shoes to my snout. "Blitz, *Riechen!*" I sniffed thoroughly, as instructed. I knew what I must do. I put my nose to the ground and started walking toward the origin of the scents. For a moment I stopped and looked at Ralph disbelievingly. Wasn't this an old familiar smell? The bells of memory were ringing loudly. The Gottlieb scent stuck to the clothes I had just sniffed. The smell of *kneidlach* in chicken soup, of chopped liver, *gefilte* fish, prayer books, and fear.

As the other dogs wandered in a somewhat confused manner, I was flooded with a wave of yearning. The joy of a forthcoming reunion passed through all my limbs and I knew exactly what I was looking for. Ralph could barely keep pace with me. I led Ralph to a house that was missing one wall. The blinds in the window had been partially torn out and were now hanging off a crooked pole. The doormat smelled exactly like the shoes Ralph had me sniff. I knew that, in a moment, the owner of the shoes would be found and I would be rewarded with petting, and perhaps a biscuit too. The pile of cardboard boxes covering half the wall at the end of the hall didn't distract me. The smell came through clearly from between the boxes. Ralph and the soldiers who accompanied us saw me hitting the boxes with my paw. No further hints were needed. There were more than ten men crowded together in the room, hidden by the pile.

Ralph and the soldiers weren't as excited by the find as I. "*Schnell! Schnell!*" They poked the men's ribs with their gun barrels, forcing them out of their hiding place. I shot a puzzled look at Ralph and didn't know what to do. The nostalgic Jewish scent spurred me to approach the stumbling men and pounce on them happily. But the aggression Ralph was displaying encouraged me to bark and growl at them. Ralph yelled at them and called them names. He even hit one with the butt of his gun. After the men I found were loaded onto the truck, Ralph took my head between his hands and kissed me on the forehead.

"Good Blitz!" he said. "You did an excellent job."

He took out more old clothes and I raced off to find what he was looking for. Barely five minutes later, I was barking at a door leading to a storeroom. Ralph acted just as roughly to the three old ladies we found sitting on the ground. I felt guilty and confused. During our training, we always received praise when we found our subject, but now the trainers' responses were cold and hostile. Did I do something wrong? I looked at Ralph, perplexed. Did I not find what you wanted? I didn't have time to deliberate any longer. A sharp familiar smell pulled me away.

"Slower, Blitz!" Ralph gasped as he tried to calm me, but the smell was so familiar and inviting that I could not be controlled. I was about to find her! It seemed as though a blend of all my puppyhood scents was waiting for me right around the corner. As though, in just a moment, I would open my eyes and find a table set for Seder night, with all the delicacies I could think of. Under a stairwell, I found two children. A young barefoot boy, and his sister who used a cane. My perplexity grew – Ralph didn't seem happy at all. Were a pair of children, just like Herschel and Reizel, not a worthy plunder in his eyes? He grabbed the girl's hair and pulled her out of the hiding place, as he cursed the boy relentlessly.

"What breed is your dog?" Jorgen Klein asked Ralph.

"I'm honestly not sure. He was brought in from the pound. He has no documentation."

Jorgen Klein petted my forehead fondly. "I think your dog found more Jews than the rest of the dogs combined."

"This dog is exceptionally smart and efficient," Ralph confirmed. "From the moment I received him, I could tell that he was exceptional. As I was washing him in the tub for the first time, I was sure he was about to jump out and cry 'Eureka!'"

Jorgen Klein smiled in agreement. "Sometimes we receive excellent dogs from the pound. I wonder how he got there. He seems used to humans. I believe he grew up in a home. . . . He must have been abandoned. I wonder if he's ever been trained."

"I don't understand how anyone could abandon such a wonderful dog. . . . There are some horrible people in the world. . . ."

"Well," Jorgen Klein said, "don't abandon him! Treat him well, and I will make sure you get a good assignment at the end of the course."

Ralph thanked him with a bow of the head.

The end of the course was nearing, and with it the pinnacle – the training competition.

The competition was divided into three parts. For the first part, we were required to jump through five hoops. The first hoop was low and required no effort. The second hoop required a light leap. The third was a jump. The fourth was already beyond the capability of the older dogs – those who hadn't stayed flexible and in shape couldn't make the jump. The fifth hoop was a real challenge. Only four dogs managed to clear the jump. Marko, the Rhodesian ridgeback, Nimitz, whose trainer explained to everyone that he was a mixed Weimaraner, Rommel, the fox terrier, and yours truly.

The second part tested our catching skills. We had to show how well we could intercept twigs and balls. It was at this point that I bade farewell to Marko. He was incredibly muscular, but not very coordinated. He would bite the air time and time again, as the items flew right past him.

For the final stage, we had to overcome the greatest obstacle of all: the wall. We had to jump over a two meter barrier. Nimitz crashed straight into it three times and was disqualified. Rommel got so excited he slipped and almost broke his teeth. Then it was my turn.

I took a deep breath and tried to calculate how many steps I'd need before I took the leap. The key to success was in starting correctly on my left leg, tilting my center of mass forward, and pushing forcefully off my right leg.

I could hear Ralph's quickened heartbeats. He was definitely more nervous than I. I ran at a calculated pace and jumped well. My front paws managed to grasp the top of the barrier. I knew that I wouldn't be able to stay in such a delicate position for long. Scratching the wall with my hind legs, I managed to raise myself and stand tall and proud at the top of the barrier. In order to heighten the drama and extend my moment of glory just a while longer, I barked several loud barks before descending the other side of the wall, winning Ralph the medal.

During the award ceremony, Ralph asked permission to show a new trick he had recently taught me. Everyone watched as Ralph whispered in my ear, "Well, Blitzy, please don't embarrass me. . . ."

I sat across from him proudly.

"*Heil Hitler!*" Ralph declared, and lifted his arm. I replied with a bark and an outstretched right paw. The entire crowd burst out laughing and the air vibrated from the effusive applause.

"Blitz, my dear," Ralph told me when we were finally alone, "Blitz my dear, you are simply a marvelous dog! You know everything before I even teach you. What can I say? You are a gift from heaven. What was I before you came along? Nothing more than a junior dog trainer in the Reich's kennel. But now. . . . Now even Jorgen Klein knows my name. I get all the praise, and I will even receive the badge of honor. But don't worry. . . . I'll always remember that at least half of the achievement is yours."

His praise was sweeping and unrestrained. I licked his face in gratitude.

"I have a little surprise for you," he said as he rolled up his sleeve. "Do you see this?"

He pointed at a new tattoo on his arm. The picture of

a dog (that looked nothing like me) with the name "Blitz" written below it.

"I did it for you!"

I must admit that I had never been honored with such a touching gesture.

Two days after the competition, our training was complete. In an impressive ceremony, an SS trainer badge was fastened to Ralph's right pocket. I received a brand new red collar, decorated in black swastikas. After the ceremony, the commander of the course gave Ralph a certificate and told him where we would serve.

Treblinka.

CHAPTER 24

The train traveled eastward. Day, night, day, night, and another day. The cars rattled as they raced down the tracks. Several dogs disembarked at each station. I was not yet dropped off. The green forests were a blur as we passed, and I could see birds flying backwards. It was the first time I had taken a train, and it wasn't a bad experience. Ralph came to the dog car several times a day to check on me and lift my spirits. The only thing that made the experience less than perfect was that we were not allowed out to relieve ourselves. It's difficult to urinate in a small cage with no privacy.

We disembarked after three days of traveling. There was a thick cloud covering the forest and it was hard to discern the barbed wire stretching behind the cypress trees. The place had a smell of finality. A point of no return. Each word, each whisper, and each echo sounded different in Treblinka. The birds' chirping sounded off-key. The air was heavy with a smell of dust that I didn't recognize. The six million scent detectors in my nose were on edge because of the mysterious smell of the place.

Upon arrival, we were welcomed by Franz Stangl, camp commandant. He wore a white riding coat, his hat in one hand and a loosely held whip in the other. He rolled the whip between his fingers and, from time to time, raised his hat to conceal a yawn. After his deputy, Kurt Franz, presented him and welcomed him with a salute, the commandant expounded his world-view to his new subordinates.

"As I see it," Hauptsturmführer Stangl said, "success is a situation where things appear to run themselves. At the end of the day, if you set ideology and missions aside, what we run here is a factory. A factory that turns Jews into ashes."

The new officers smiled and watched their silver-tongued commandant in adoration.

"Things running themselves," the commandant continued, "means that each member of the senior staff knows his job perfectly, and all that's left for me to do is supervise from afar and make sure nothing goes wrong."

Stangl's adjutant came in, saluted hastily, and handed the commandant a note. Stangl took a moment to read the note, placed it in his pocket, and went on. "After weeks of hard work, I believe I have managed to bring Treblinka to its desired status. And I want to tell you it wasn't easy, but it was certainly worth it, because I sleep well at night. I sleep well because I have a senior staff that I trust. A senior staff thanks to whom our factory is flourishing."

After the commandant spoke, it was the deputy's turn. Instead of boring us with more words, Oberscharführer Kurt Franz wished to show us a demonstration. We followed him to the marching grounds. As we arrived, the prisoners who had been taken from their work were ushered in with whips.

Oberscharführer Franz surveyed the lines of prisoners with squinted eyes. He walked along the front row, back and forth, holding a whip over his shoulder. His silence did not bode well.

"You know exactly what your friends did," the deputy commandant said, removing his pistol from its holster. "If someone is whipped, it is because he deserved it! And when I command to count out the lashes, I *will* be obeyed. . . ." As he spoke, he put the pistol to the head of one of the prisoners. "We don't have much sympathy here for jewelry thieves either. . . ." The gun moved to the head of the next prisoner. "And there is only one punishment," he said as he pointed the gun at a third prisoner, "for attempted escape!"

I heard a gunshot for the first time in my life. Three corpses of Jews lay before me. I planted my feet firmly on the ground, fearing that if I did not, my panic would betray me and I would bolt. I glanced at the experienced dogs. The sound of the shots did not impress them. Their composure reassured me. I was moved by the ease with which man holds life and death in his hands! I now fully accepted the supremacy of man. There is no creature in the world that can stand up against him. The Jews' last twitches were unnerving. Despite myself, I looked away. Neither the sight of the dead cat in the Rosenpark nor the sight of my pack mates succumbing to disease reached this level of horror. I thought once again of the question I had asked myself in my very first days on Earth. This time the answer was firm – no! Dogs and humans are not one and the same. And

I, though I understand man and his ways and am fluent in his tongue – I am a dog. This fact was clear to me beyond any shade of doubt. A dog I was born and a dog I would die.

Although dogs do not come within a mile of man's cruelty, some of Kurt Franz's cruelty seemed to rub off on his dog. Kurt would wander the camp accompanied by his dog, Barry. Barry was a huge black creature with long, curly fur. As long as his sadistic owner was nowhere to be seen, Barry was a pleasant dog, easygoing and very polite. Kurt's presence would instill in him murderous tendencies, and on command he would pounce on the designated Jew, sinking his sharp teeth in the poor Jew's genitals.

But Barry wasn't the deadliest dog in the camp: in all the areas of bloodthirstiness, aggression, and vitality, Mensch surpassed him tenfold. Mensch, the speckled dog that belonged to August Miete, camp sergeant. I didn't know it, but I was destined yet to meet that dog in a fight to the death. Anyone would be sick to their stomach seeing that dog. Mensch wouldn't let go of his prey until he tore its flesh into bits. He would walk around camp holding a shoe that he had ripped off one of his victims, the sole attached by only a few threads. The sole would dangle as though its tormented soul was asking for redemption.

Mensch would send me bored looks and bark impatiently.

His cocky barks got on my nerves. I hate dogs that bark *Hochdeutsch*.

Mensch's owner, August Miete, could be recognized by

the large knife he carried on his belt. He would spend the greater part of his time sitting in the marching grounds sharpening his knife with a rock. Mensch would sit at his feet and together they would ambush the passing Jews.

One evening, as I was on a walk with Ralph, we passed by the grounds. The grating sound of the blade against the rock could be heard from afar.

"*Guten abend*," Ralph greeted August Miete.

Mensch wasn't there, to my great pleasure. I wasn't in the mood for a barking match.

Miete raised his eyes and replied, "I've been looking for you. Listen, if you want to make shitloads of money, my dog against yours. . . . The stinking Ukrainians will pay good money to see a fight. We can make some profit, and not just any profit. . . . There is serious money in this. What do you say?"

"No, that's not our thing. That's not what I trained Blitz for," Ralph replied. "Blitz isn't a fight dog. The Ukrainians' money doesn't interest me."

"'The Ukrainians' money doesn't interest me . . .'" Miete imitated Ralph. "Money interests us all. You're just scared that Franz will catch you. So what if he does? What will he do to us? So he'll write another comment in my service file – I don't give a rat's ass about his comments. A man can't live off the money they pay us here."

"Leave it be," Ralph pleaded. "I don't want a part in these fights."

"Afraid of the fight, huh?" Miete stopped sharpening his knife for a moment. "You're scared! You're scared for your stupid dog! Cowards like you will lose us this war!"

Miete hissed an expletive between his teeth and we continued on our walk.

"Because of lowlifes like him," Ralph told me, "I'm not so sure anymore that we deserve to win. . . ." He filled his lungs with a deep breath and looked at me tenderly. "Ach, Blitzy Blitz. What would I do here without you? It's like you're the only human being in this place."

I tried to pull him toward the prisoners' barracks. A strange sound was coming from one of the shacks. It reminded me of the ticking of a sewing machine.

"*Bei Fuß!*" Ralph commanded, bothered by the taut leash.

I obeyed, coming back to his side.

"If you want to run a little," Ralph explained, "you don't have to dislocate my shoulder. You just have to ask."

He let me off my leash and I ran toward the barracks to find out what the mysterious ticking noise was. I suddenly smelled a strange mixture of scents: the scent of Jews and the scent of mustiness. I entered the shack that the smells were originating from and was enchanted by the magnitude of my find – a huge warehouse filled with shoes. How wonderful! I will snatch a little shoe for myself. Then I can also hold a shoe in my mouth and walk around camp as though I own the world.

A strange vapor arose from the pile.

I heard the voice of the Heavenly Dog, **"Your brothers' blood cries out to me from the mound."**

I retreated, my tail standing on end.

CHAPTER 25

One morning before sunrise, before I could distinguish between dog and wolf, a trill was heard from the whistle of Otto Stadie, the camp's head of administration. It was a sign that a train full of fresh victims was about to pull in from the town. It would arrive at the gate in just a few minutes. Ralph hurried me, wanting to catch our usual spot at the very front of the platform.

I hoped there would be many Jews on this train. The previous trains had come in with very few. Accordingly, the plundered food I received was just as limited.

The tracks trembled and the locomotive poked through the morning mist. The train came to a stop with a dull screech and its heavy doors opened. Thousands of tattered Jews fell out of the train cars, steered by whips. I carried out my job efficiently and barked loudly at any Jew that stepped out of line.

When all the Jews were standing in a tight group in the middle of the platform, everyone was hushed, and Otto Stadie made a reassuring announcement through his megaphone. Soon everyone would be showered and disinfected.

They would receive new clothes and be sent to a labor camp. The elderly and ill were requested to accompany him to the *lazaret* for medical treatment. Men between the ages of eighteen and thirty were commanded to separate from the rest of the group and report to the courtyard, arranged in groups of five.

I was ordered to stand watch over this group of young men in the courtyard.

My nostrils were suddenly electrified by a familiar odor. My heart skipped a beat, my ears reached straight into the air, and my tail went taut. Could I be hallucinating? What was this aromatic mirage? Was I being tricked by an illusion? I focused my gaze. There, in the group forming lines in the courtyard, I recognized Joshua Gottlieb, now a young man.

Ralph felt my tail wagging and couldn't understand what I was excited about.

Joshua stood with the group of men, in the middle of the rightmost row.

Suddenly Joshua noticed me, confusion evident on his face. Could it be?

The cruel SS officer, Joseph Hirtreiter, approached Joshua from behind and grabbed the back of his neck.

"What do you think you're looking at?" Hirtreiter shouted, raising his arm to hit him. "Stupid Jude!"

Joshua didn't dare shield his head with his hands, and took the blow in all its strength. I suddenly became a wild, uncontrollable dog. A fearless Jewish dingo. Who was this mongrel, I thought as my blood boiled in my veins, who dared to raise a hand against my puppyhood friend? I charged forward like a bat out of hell. Ralph lost his grip on my leash. I leapt with great force, mouth wide open, prepared to bite. I brought Joseph Hirtreiter to the ground and tightened my jaws on his face in blind anger.

I was now positive that Joshua recognized me, but he was wise enough not to disclose our long relationship. Ralph came running and kicked me forcefully. I rolled over on the cement and muffled a yelp. Ralph helped the injured Joseph back onto his feet.

"I don't know what's gotten into this stupid dog," Ralph apologized. "He's never acted so idiotically."

"He's a sick dog! Psychotic!" Joseph cried, resting a hand on his mauled face. He glanced back at his hands, now painted with his own blood, and yelled, "He should be shot in the head!"

Ralph saw Joseph Hirtreiter reaching for his holster and quickly protected me with his own body.

"It's just a few small cuts," Ralph downplayed the four holes my fangs had made in Joseph Hirtreiter's ugly face.

"I'm bleeding! Your bloody dog bit me! I should empty my entire magazine into his head right now! He's a crazy dog and he should be put down!"

"You're wrong, sir . . ." Joshua tried to intervene. Joseph Hirtreiter looked at Joshua with disbelieving eyes. Then he delivered a painful lash directly to his face. Woe to the Jew who tells an SS officer that he is wrong.

There was nothing in the world that I wanted more than to tear open Joseph Hirtreiter's carotid artery, but I fully grasped that another attack would kill both me and Joshua.

Shivering from fear, with two broken teeth, Joshua fumbled on the ground searching for his fallen glasses. One of the lenses had shattered. Joshua put on his broken spectacles, gathered his courage, and addressed the Nazi. "Herr officer held me by the scruff of the neck, as puppies are held. Dogs are shepherds by nature. The dog thought you were trying to remove one of the sheep from the herd – he was simply doing his job."

I looked at Joshua's broken teeth. A day would come, I thought, that I would avenge those two teeth. Ralph, who was an expert on canine behavior, recognized the insightfulness of Joshua's observation.

Hirtreiter was relentless. "Herr Ralph Schmidt," he threatened my trainer in a hiss, "the dog is crazy and he must be killed."

"The dog is fine," Ralph defended me.

But Joseph, who outranked Ralph, yelled furiously, "I told you to kill the bastard! Kill it! Kill! Kill!"

Es iz geven geshribn oif zayn naz – it was written all over his snout – he was evil through and through. Embers of hatred shone in his eyes.

"Sir," Joshua said to Ralph, "sir, if I may, I can prove that the dog is definitely in his right mind, and very bright as well." Ralph looked surprised, and implored Joseph with his eyes to allow it.

"Come on, little Jude, come on and prove it!" Joseph said, and added menacingly, "But if I don't like your proof, you and the dog are both. . . ." He drew his finger across his neck.

"Stand across from the dog," Joshua told Ralph. "Close your eyes, and hate him. Loathe him in your thoughts, just as you loathe your most mortal enemy."

Joseph stood on the side looking skeptical, and caressed his pistol.

The moment I sensed the scent of hatred coming from my trainer, I lay on the ground and began whimpering. I scratched the ground with my claws, showing my submission. Ralph opened one eye and squinted at me in disbelief at my telepathic powers.

"Now love him! Love him with all your heart and with all your might!"

I could feel the love bursting from Ralph, and I ran toward him happily, wagging my tail.

"Hate him!" Joshua cried, and Ralph, his eyes still shut, scrunched his face in cold hatred. The scent of loathing and alienation saddened me greatly and I began crawling backwards, heartbreak in my eyes.

"Love him again!"

I jumped on Ralph and licked his chin.

Joseph snorted scornfully at Ralph. "Just wait and see, you and your Jude will. . . ."

One of Kurt Franz's lackeys came running and interrupted him, standing tall at attention.

"Oberscharführer said that all senior staff must report to the briefing room in twenty minutes."

Joseph replied that he would be there, and Ralph nodded his acknowledgement.

After Joseph was gone, Ralph told Joshua that he had never seen such an eye-opening demonstration of a dog understanding his owner. He promised that he would try to appoint Joshua to feed the animals and clean their cages.

CHAPTER 26

Joshua lived in a tiny shack near the kennels. Every morning after roll call, he would take a box of leftovers from the cook and divide whatever the Germans had left from their meals between me and my friends. After we'd dine, I would join him as he spread breadcrumbs for the chickens and the ducks. The carrot peels, onions, and potatoes he kept for the three strange animals that lived in the small pen between the warehouses. This corner was the quietest place in the camp, and that is where Ralph would conduct my morning training.

"Good morning, little piggies," Joshua would greet them. "I've brought you yummy food." Joshua seemed to be very fond of these three chubby creatures, and I liked them too. Joshua called the littlest one Maulwurf, the one with pudgy cheeks Springy, and the third, who was a little yellowish, he called Zanfi.

Springy and Maulwurf would approach him immediately and put their snouts in the box of slops. Zanfi preferred to walk up to me and suck up a little bit of my face in his snout. I would answer his funny welcome with a friendly bark, and he would bark a funny little bark back, "oink oink!"

Zanfi was somewhat squashed and incredibly lazy, but he had a sharp look in his eyes and was very clever. One morning, I learned just how astute he was. Ralph was trying to teach me a new trick. First he sat me down and commanded *"Bleib!"* Then he would walk away, and signal to me to walk toward him, but each time he called *"Platz!"* I had to stop and lie down, with my stomach flat on the ground. I admit, the maneuver was complex and confusing, and it took a lot of practice until I understood exactly what Ralph wanted. To my astonishment, I noticed that while I was busy learning, my friend Zanfi was imitating each move from the other side of the fence. He was also learning to follow Ralph's commands. In fact, I think he learned the procedure faster than I.

Upon learning how bright Zanfi was, I would join Joshua every morning for the feeding, in order to visit my friend and see how he was doing. After he finished his rounds, Joshua would go to the corner of his living quarters, and underneath his bed he'd place a little bit of the bread that he withheld from the duck, and a little food that he kept out of my friends' dishes. He hid the food in order to feed his bedmates: Yomtov, Lerman, Valovanchik, and Salzburg.

Lerman was a bald Jew with a huge nose and a pair of oval nostrils that would quiver every time he cried bitterly. Two fresh scars on the sides of his head indicated that his side locks had been cruelly shorn off. He would mutter passages of prayer for hours on end. "Out of the depths I cry to you, Lord / I called upon the Lord in distress / Rise up, Lord, and let thine enemies be scattered / Avenge before our eyes the spilled blood of Your servants." But why did he repeat his prayer so? Was it a sign that God was not hearing his prayer?

Salzburg was broad-shouldered, his forehead furrowed and his eyes bulging. Hidden under his bed were pictures of him as a happy family man with a rounded belly and a double chin. His belly, extra chin, and family were all gone now. He had buried his wife and two daughters, and would mourn them often. He refused to let them go, and would often say things like "If my wife were here, she would no doubt . . ." or "Just like my girls would say. . . ."

Valovanchik was lively and nimble. He was a man of action, and a smooth talker as well.

One evening he told his friends in a broken voice, "Four years I spent in the army there. . . . I was the youngest officer in the entire Siberian battalion. All my soldiers are gone now; I saw each and every one of them take a bullet. . . ."

He would scream in his sleep, and his friends would wake him and cool his face with a shred of damp cloth. He carried a letter in his pocket and would glance at it often.

"What is that letter?" his friends would ask, but he would lower his gaze and shove the letter back into his pocket.

"I think we can escape if we plan it properly," he would say.

"You think that prisoners with no strength or weapons can overpower German soldiers?" Lerman would ask. "And how exactly do you plan to get over the electric fence? And how will you avoid the Ukrainian soldiers and the dogs?"

Valovanchik did not respond, but his face was determined and there was a scent about him that I knew very well – the scent of revenge.

At night, Joshua would divide the food he'd managed to steal between his friends.

Valovanchik chewed on the edge of a bone and hummed marching tunes.

"Ach," Salzburg said fondly, "my wife knew how to make bread like this."

Lerman was always careful to wash his hands ritually before eating bread. At times, though, he was forced to rub his hands with dirt because there was no water available. After he ate some leftover pie, a quarter of a piece of bread, and a little bit of meat still stuck to a fish skeleton, he would close his eyes and say the Grace after Meals. He would begin his blessing with "You give them their food at the proper time" and end with "I have never seen the righteous forsaken."

One evening, the three friends waited for Joshua to return from his work in the kennels and share with them his daily tithe. What was keeping him? Footfalls were heard outside the shack and the three went to the door and peeked out to see if Joshua had finally arrived.

It was not Joshua.

"Good evening, Herr Galveski," Valovanchik welcomed the man, who entered pushing a loaded wheelbarrow. "What are you carrying in there?"

"Building debris," Galveski replied. "It's very important to clear the debris."

Valovanchik nodded in agreement.

The wheelbarrow smelled of oil and steel.

"Don't forget to move the large sacks of potatoes," Valovanchik said.

"I won't forget," Galveski promised. "Everything will be moved in time."

CHAPTER 27

As the sunset reached its most picturesque point, with half the sun above the horizon and half below, Ralph and the commandant arrived at the kennel. Ralph had gotten on the commandant's good side. When they finished their dinner together, they brought the leftovers to the dogs. Joshua, standing at attention, received the plate of leftovers from Ralph's hands.

"Tell the dogs *guten appetite*," Ralph joked. "I made the chicken pot pie myself!"

"Yes, sir," Joshua confirmed.

"And bring me Blitz. I want Blitz to join the commandant and me on an evening stroll."

"Yes, sir."

As Joshua let me out of my cage and untied my leash, Franz Stangl and Ralph pulled out cigarettes. The commandant wiggled a lighter out of his pocket and lit the end of Ralph's cigarette.

"Blitzy, Blitzy, Blitz!" Ralph called when he saw how excited I was to see him. Ralph tapped on his shirt pockets and, in accordance with our sign language, I stood on my hind legs and rested my paws lightly on his chest. I greeted him with a lick.

"This is my kind of dog," Ralph told his commandant. "And this Jew takes good care of him!"

Franz Stangl was impressed.

"Take a cigarette," Ralph said, extending his pack to Joshua.

Joshua was surprised by the gesture. He didn't know what was more dangerous – taking the cigarette or refusing it. He gathered his courage and drew a cigarette from the pack that was offered to him.

We walked on together, the three of us: Ralph, the commandant, and myself. A pleasant evening stroll.

"Is there any special reason," the commandant asked, "that you are so fond of the Jew?"

They walked at a leisurely pace, heading toward the east fence.

"He takes good care of the dogs. . . . Yes, he knows how to take care of dogs."

"And is it your common practice to offer cigarettes to Jews?" There was a hint of suspicion in the commandant's question.

"It was a one-time gesture," Ralph assured him. Trying to further justify his behavior, he added, "But he really does work well, and in any case, he'll be shot in the head in just a few weeks."

The commandant smiled. Ralph's simplicity pleased him. The warm summer evening and the sweet smell in the air helped make the atmosphere feel casual. I think my presence also contributed to the sense of camaraderie. They watched the clouds as the sun lit them ablaze.

"This is the scenery for a revelation," the commandant said.

Ralph answered with a silent nod.

The commandant leaned toward me and petted my head. "Usually," he confessed to Ralph, "I don't really get along with dogs. When I was a child, a dog bit me, and since then I've been a little scared of them."

"You certainly have no reason to be scared of Blitz."

"He also smells good," Franz Stangl added. "Usually dogs have an unpleasant smell. You know what I mean. When you enter a house with a dog, you can smell it right away."

"Yes, he smells excellent. The Jew washed him this morning. He gave him a shower and used lots of soap, just as he should!"

"Does the dog enjoy showers?"

"Blitz? No, I don't think he particularly enjoys that process."

"Maybe he's Jewish," Hauptsturmführer Stangl said.

Ralph looked at him, puzzled.

"You know," the commandant said, hardly containing his laughter, "the Jews don't exactly enjoy our showers."

Smiles spread across their faces as they walked, and Franz's eyes took on a nostalgic glitter. "You young folk won't understand it. It's hard to explain today how people used to look at you when you said, 'I'm leaving everything and dedicating my life to the party.'"

Ralph looked at the commandant for an explanation.

"It was the joy of eating fruit from the forbidden tree – joining a party that was still illegal."

"Things today are simpler," Ralph agreed.

"I felt like a babe thrown into deep water – either you

learned how to swim or you drowned. But today I believe that is the most effective method. He who hesitates is lost. I'm telling you, the moment I was asked to participate in the Euthanasia program, I knew: now I officially belonged to the founding generation. Ach, those were the days. . . ."

He lit another cigarette.

"And what are the dog's special qualities?"

"Ho," Ralph's eyes shone, "he's the smartest dog I've ever met. He understands everything. Just everything. It's like he has a dictionary in his head. I think that if he were able to speak, he would be able to have an intelligent conversation with any elementary school graduate. I think he's brighter than most of our Ukrainians."

"Well," the commandant said, looking at me fondly, "that's barely an impressive feat. I think the porcupines that vandalize my lettuce gardens at night have a fighting chance against the Ukrainians' intelligence."

The two laughed in a typically restrained German manner.

As the commandant laughed with his subordinate, the barriers of rank began to crack and the two spoke like equals.

"Let me compliment you," Franz Stangl said. "This is something I don't usually say. You should know, from the first day I received command of this camp, I've kept a diary. It's a personal diary and I write an entry every evening. I want to tell you that you are mentioned in my diary more than once or twice, and it's always a positive mention. You focus on completing the assignments that you were recruited for. You aren't like Sergeant Küttner and Kurt

Franz, those brown-nosers. I'll tell you quite frankly – I have a lot of respect for folks like you."

Ralph blushed.

The commandant seemed pleased at Ralph's bashfulness. It strengthened his sense of patronage. He conversed with Ralph in a friendly, personal manner.

"So what do you intend to do after the war?"

Ralph remained silent and pondered. The war was reality. Post-war times were post-reality – better left unconsidered.

Eventually he spoke in a decisive voice that surprised even himself. "I want to learn engineering. Or maybe theology."

The commandant gave him a quizzical look.

"I'm not religious, but theology seems to be an interesting and worthy pursuit."

"You don't want to continue working as a trainer?"

"My father, may he rest in peace, was a locomotive engineer. He took part in constructing the first train from Berlin to Düsseldorf. And my grandfather was an important theologian. I would like to continue in one of the family paths."

"My father passed away when I was fifteen," the commandant said. "I remember him well. I'm so sorry he can't see me now. My father was never in Germany."

"He never visited Germany?" Ralph asked, disbelieving. For a moment he was taken aback by his own spontaneity.

The commandant was not ruffled by the question. "Not even once. He never got to see the great Germany in its glory days. A Germany spread over all of Europe."

"Speaking of which, what *is* the latest news from the

front?" Ralph tried to divert the conversation to a less personal topic.

"I'm afraid I don't know much more than you do. It seems things there are not so simple. But I'll tell you this: war and victory are all in the head. Listen to me," the commandant said, walking slowly with his hands clasped behind his back. "If the soldiers are determined and the commanders are not afraid to give orders – victory is just a matter of time."

Ralph looked alert.

"That doesn't mean that war is a simple thing. These Soviets are stubborn. You don't have to be a genius to see it. The Slavs are inferior, but stubborn as mules. A few bombs aren't enough to beat them. We have to break them completely. That's it!"

Ralph looked like he wanted to hear more, but his commandant was tired of military talk. "Why should we exhaust ourselves trying to fix all the Reich's problems when we have plenty of our own here?"

The two continued walking, but the conversation dwindled down. The evening stroll was almost over.

"Well," the commandant said, trying to cover a yawn, "we have two trains coming in tomorrow morning. What do you say, time to return the dog to his kennel?"

It was, of course, a rhetorical question.

Ralph returned me to my cage just as Joshua was walking out of the kennel toward his shack. Joshua, who was caught off guard by our return, jumped to attention. A steak bone fell from his sleeve.

"The little Jew is stealing the food we brought for the dogs," Ralph whispered, astonished. "And I thought I had seen it all."

Ralph caught Joshua by the sleeve and dragged him toward the *lazaret*. "How dare you! No wonder the dogs are hungry and bark all night." More pieces of meat and fish dropped from Joshua's stained shirt.

I strode by Ralph's side upon command. Although dogs are not accustomed to praying, I looked up to the sky. *Where are you, Heavenly Dog,* I thought as I gazed at the black sky that silently watched us from above. *Now you command me to escort Joshua, my own flesh and blood, to the pit of death?*

Ralph ordered Joshua to stand on the wooden plank at the rim of the pit. There was an eternal flame burning between the plaster-covered bodies that lay one upon the other. Ralph aimed his gun. *I must pounce again,* my stomach shrunk in pain, *to bite! To tear! To stab! To destroy any threat on Joshua's life.* But I was paralyzed. How could I bite the hand that feeds me? How could I pierce the arm that had been tattooed just for me? Could I really harm Ralph, my pride and joy? I was a coward. I knew that if I charged, I would be shot myself. I accepted the verdict with a stiff upper lip. My tongue cleaved to the roof of my mouth, preventing me from barking. *Heavenly Dog, save us!* A weak whimper escaped my mouth, quieter even than the faintest wail of the *shofar. Heavenly Dog, save us.*

"I give you a cigarette," Ralph said, and shifted his grip on the pistol, "and you spit at me. You should be ashamed of yourself, you dirty Jude."

"I'm ashamed of nothing, sir." Joshua looked Ralph straight in the eye. "And have no doubt – if I had to choose between a fate among the Jews in that pit or among the Germans pulling the trigger – I would choose the pit."

Ralph's face whitened from Joshua's fearlessness as he stared down the barrel of a gun. I was just as astonished.

"There's another thing that you should hear before you pull that trigger. All these weeks that I've been taking care of Blitz, as you call him, I haven't been taking care of your dog, I've been taking care of mine. I've known this dog since he was the size of a rat. He was born on March 31, 1935, on the carpet of the house I was evicted from by your damned Nazi friends when I was nineteen. When you praised me for taking such good care of your dog, I felt like I didn't deserve your praise; this dog is as dear as a brother to me. I raised him from his very first day on Earth. He had five siblings; one of them died within just a few days. If you don't believe me, the dog's mother still lives with our old housekeeper. The housekeeper's name is Matilda Schwartzschpiln, and the dog's mother is Bruriah."

When I heard my mother's name, my ears perked up.

Ralph slipped a cigarette out of his pocket. There was no doubt in his heart that the Jew spoke the truth. He lit his cigarette and took three deep puffs. The cloud of smoke that covered his face slowly dissipated. He gazed for a long moment at the edge of the cigarette that was slowly being consumed. Then he threw the butt into the pit. He aimed his gun at a nearby discarded bottle and shot. Shot and missed. He missed the second shot, too. The third bullet hit the bottle and it shattered noisily.

"So what is this dog's name?"

"Caleb. Don't ask me why. My little sister Reizel chose it. And she . . . well, you can't exactly ask her why anymore."

Joshua's shoulders began to tremble.

"So your name is Caleb," my beloved trainer said, as he

kneeled down beside me. "Come Caleb," Ralph uttered my real name. "Come Caleb, let's return you to your cage."

Joshua remained standing by the pit for a long time. Stars appeared in the dark sky and a silent cold wind blew between the barbed-wire fences. The multitude of stars made my existence seem fleeting.

Just before midnight, a gunshot rang through the silence of the night.

It was the last time I saw Ralph.

CHAPTER 28

*R*alph was replaced by a new trainer named Sebastian. He had a sharp, hooked nose that had been broken in one of the many fights he had gotten into. Yellow stubble grew sparsely and in an unkempt fashion around his small mouth and clenched jaw. He had round eyes, and reeked of cigarettes and alcohol.

All the dogs in the kennel hated Sebastian. Even his friends were appalled by his training methods.

"Beat the dog until it bleeds. Let the hound fear the Germans and take its anger out on Jews."

He would lift the new puppies in the kennel by their ears and whip them raw. We were afraid to bark in protest, for it would only anger him more and double the lashes he dealt out.

One day Sebastian entered Joshua's shack.

"Listen up, Jew!" he ordered Joshua. "From now until tomorrow afternoon, I forbid you to feed Blitz."

Joshua stood and replied, "Yes, sir."

Sebastian looked from side to side, his pupils dilated. He smelled like beer.

"Tomorrow we'll teach that bragging Miete whose dog is strongest in the camp. Oh, he'll learn that tomorrow."

Joshua, who had stood so bravely at the pit of death, now turned white with fear.

"Sir," he addressed Sebastian, shaking, "does the officer intend to have the dog participate in a fight?"

"Why do you ask?" Sebastian shot back, his long neck extending further out of his shirt. "Do you have a problem with that?" He rested his hand on the butt of his pistol. "Do you intend to rat me out?"

"No, sir," Joshua replied. "Of course not. I won't tell anyone. I just wanted to say that this dog fights best when he's sated. If you want him to win, you have to give him good food."

"Fights best when sated, eh?" His neck retracted back into his shirt, he let go of his pistol, and rubbed his hands together. "I'll get him a good meal!"

The next afternoon, Sebastian entered the kennel and instructed Joshua to put on my leash. He walked me to the staff housing yard and placed a platter covered with a cloth before me. The magical smell of well-prepared meat arose from the platter.

"Listen up!" he said to me, pointing at the food. "If you need good food to fight, you'll get as much as you want. Here, I arranged a fantastic meal for you. Last night, we had a party for Kurt Franz, and I saved this especially for you. I want you to eat fast and fight like a lion!" He removed the cloth from the platter and revealed the feast. Propped up on the tray, with a plum in his mouth, was Zanfi's head. I approached, seized by nausea, and sniffed my roasted friend.

Barely an hour after I finished my feast we stood, Mensch and I, face to face in the fenced vegetable patch near the German staff housing.

The bloodthirsty Ukrainians descended from the watchtowers and bet everything they had in their pockets. August Miete and Kurt Franz, who had arranged the fight, set the odds at one-to-ten in Mensch's favor. One Ukrainian named Tichowicz gave Miete two hundred Reichsmarks and five golden coins, betting on me.

"You'll see," he dared joke at the expense of Joseph Hirtreiter, who had also come to watch the fight. "He'll bring all his enemies to their knees, just as he brought Hirtreiter to his."

Joseph Hirtreiter thought otherwise.

"Just you wait, you soft-brained Ukrainian. You'll soon be parting with your money, just as this bedeviled dog will be parting with his life. This will be his grave."

Mensch yanked the metal chains that were hooked onto his collar. He trampled the potato patch in his murderous excitement, and crushed the zucchini and carrots with his far-reaching paws.

Tichowicz wasn't impressed, and he unlatched a lavish wristwatch from his left arm.

"I'll bet this, too!"

I wanted to thank him for his boundless faith.

Miete assessed the worth of the watch and wrote it down.

Mensch, who was an experienced fight dog, stood ready to pounce. He barked continuously and prepared himself to deliver deadly bites. I barked back just as loudly, but deep down I feared that my bark was worse than my bite. Mensch was bigger and stronger, his jaws more powerful than mine, and nothing would ease his terrible temper but blood. An important fact made my bad feeling even worse – Joshua wasn't there! I looked in every direction, but there was no sign of Joshua. He must have preferred not to watch me die.

One of the junior SS officers ran to his room and came back with a camera. Mensch and I were both memorialized in our last minutes before the fight.

Sergeant Miete read out the bets and summarized the rules of the fight: the dog that leaves the arena alive will be declared the winner. He held his whistle in his hand, ready to mark the start of the fight. I had not yet decided whether I was better off fighting in the center of the arena or staying close to the fence. Should I try to bite his heels, or look for the weak points in his neck? If I had been granted a little longer to prepare for the fight, my chances would have been much better. Maybe I'd be best off biting myself to death, falling on my own sword, to become a legend throughout the canine world.

Sergeant Miete placed the whistle in his mouth. The Ukrainians around the fence elbowed and shouldered their way to the front.

A sharp whistle sounded.

Mensch charged straight for my neck. He aimed for a clean and quick conclusion. I barely had time to move my head. His fang sunk into my shoulder. I forced myself to remain silent, knowing that if he knew how much it hurt, it would simply fuel his murderousness. We rolled together, raising clouds of dust. I stretched the upper half of my body as far as it would go and managed to catch his front right paw between my teeth. I strengthened my grip and Mensch stumbled. I dragged him onto his back. If I hadn't been so busy surviving, I would have taken a moment to thank my brother, who had tried that trick on me over and over again when we were young, and my mother, who had refused to rebuke him. Mensch the Terrible let out a whimper of pain and retreated slightly.

"So that's what you're about, you son of a bitch?" his look said. "You can't fight like a dog, so you play dirty?"

I hoped his leg injury was more serious than it looked, but I saw no indication of a limp in his stride.

He charged again. This time his fangs landed deep in my throat. The Ukrainians sighed, disappointed – it was ending faster than they had expected. One of them made a joke about the foolish Tichowicz. That's it, I thought resignedly. In a moment, he will shake his head and my neck will break. In just one moment, I will meet the same fate as the black cat between Karl Gustav's jaws. And I, just like that kitten, would die with my eyes open. But I was wrong. He was in no hurry. Mensch tried to prolong his pleasure and looked at me through squinted eyes, trying to suck every drop of sadistic pleasure out of my desperate position. *This is it!* I thought. *The last moment of weakness is within reach.* I stretched out my foot and stabbed him in the eye with an extended claw. A whimper of pain squeezed from his throat. His grip loosened and he retreated to the edge of the arena with his tail between his legs. Blood was pouring from his pupil. Tichowicz began to clap, and shot back jokes at those who had mocked him. I felt satisfied. I had justified his faith in me. Even if I died, it would be a hero's death. My shoulder was in great pain, and the pain radiated to my stomach. Mensch rose and steadied himself on his four feet. He recovered quickly and growled. He had reached his limit – he was seeing red. The Ukrainians in the crowd were out of their minds. They had never seen such a balanced and well-fought match. Joseph Hirtreiter and Sergeant Miete cheered Mensch on. Tichowicz was on my side. "Get up! Charge!" he called to me. "Rip the vermin to pieces!"

And then . . . a volley of shots was heard.

"They shot Sergeant Küttner!" The shouts echoed from every corner of the camp. "Sergeant Küttner has been shot!" Trucks started driving, rifles were loaded, and the machine guns on the watchtowers shot long bursts of fire. The crowd looked around in confusion and tried to assess the situation.

A low-ranking Ukrainian with thick sideburns, whose fingers were covered in looted rings, came running and reported: "Sergeant Küttner, commandant of the lower camp, was found in the courtyard drowning in his own blood."

"Who shot him?" Joseph Hirtreiter asked.

"The Jews!" answered the Ukrainian.

It was the opening shot of the prisoners' revolt. I would later hear the story over and over from Joshua and his friends. An unlucky disruption had almost ruined the whole plan: Oberscharführer Küttner appeared in the area of the prisoners' shacks. He entered one of the shacks searching for Kuba the Snitch. Armed with knives and Molotov cocktails, Joshua and his friends watched from a safe distance as Kuba, the oldest prisoner and a notorious snitch, entered the shack after Küttner and talked to him for several minutes.

Joshua and his friends knew that Kuba would sell out his own mother for a cigarette butt. They assumed he had sniffed out the unrest and was quick to report to his patrons.

Salzburg turned to Yomtov Lerman and ordered him to report the meeting between Kuba and Küttner to the leaders of the revolt. He asked for a pistol on the double. Lerman departed with Salzburg's request, and Küttner exited the shack, eyeing the area suspiciously.

He called over a young prisoner who was wandering the grounds without permission, and searched him. In the prisoner's clothes he found money notes that he had prepared for the escape. Küttner began beating the youth mercilessly.

Salzburg and Joshua feared that Küttner would draw out information about the revolt plans from the young prisoner, using violence and torture. As they spoke in hushed voices, Valovanchik, who was a member of the underground, arrived holding a pistol.

"He's taking him to the torture chamber," Salzburg whispered to his armed friend. "He'll do anything to find out why he was hiding money in his clothes." Valovanchik didn't need another hint. He left his hiding place and shot Küttner, leaving him to bleed.

The gunshot lit the fire of the uprising, saving me from the final round of my fight against Mensch. Wielding axes, knives, pistols, and grenades, the prisoners now rose against their wardens. The fuel warehouse was set ablaze. Its fierce flames spread to the nearby buildings. A long chain of explosions shook the camp.

The Germans ran, frightened, from the buildings that had not yet caught fire, as the Ukrainians atop the watchtowers held a fierce firefight with the prisoners. Everyone ran to the fences, trampling their wounded brethren.

Where is Joshua? I ran to and fro in the chaos, trying to find him.

There! Joshua was running to the fence like the rest. He was about to jump. Did he intend to abandon me? I barked loudly.

Joshua recognized my bark, turned around and called, "Come, Caleb! Come!"

As the fire of the uprising blazed, as bullets whistled over my head, my name was returned to me. My childhood name was now forever returned to me.

I saw Mensch racing toward Joshua. I galloped toward him, ignoring the stabbing pains in my shoulder. I had to get there before Mensch did, no matter what. At the very last second, I caught his tail between my teeth. Mensch tried to jump backwards and bite me back, but he stumbled over his own paws. With a fierce shake, I threw him against the fence. His paw got caught between the barbs, his fur stood unnaturally on end, and his eyes almost came out of their sockets. His mouth opened and sparks danced between his fangs. His body shivered and shook until his head fell, bowing before death.

I could practically see the scythe of death on Mensch's throat as he lay stiff on the ground, but we weren't safe yet. Vialich, a cowardly Ukrainian who would have gladly apprenticed for the devil, aimed his gun at Joshua. I leapt with all my strength and clamped my jaws around his face. My tongue was submerged in the fresh taste of enemy blood.

I spit the tip of his nose to the ground and he fell back, dropping his gun and holding his bleeding stump.

"You'll pay for this!" he shouted, as he unsheathed a sharp knife from his belt.

You're scaring the fleas off of me, I thought angrily, and prepared for another pounce.

"Come, Caleb! Come!" Joshua called.

I hesitated for one moment.

Joshua motioned toward an opening in the fence and called me again. "Come, Caleb! Now!" I left the injured Ukrainian and ran toward the opening. On my way there, I stepped in a patch of cement that hadn't yet dried. To this day anyone who visits Treblinka can see my paw print in the cement – a silent witness to what happened in the camp that day.

Long live liberty! I thought as we ran, Joshua and I, among the prisoners fleeing as fast as they could from the burning camp.

CHAPTER 29

*A*t first we all ran together. Then we split up and continued running in smaller groups. Ukrainian horsemen were at our heels. Some prisoners didn't have the strength to run on. The Ukrainians shot them until their bullets ran out, and then began stabbing escapees with their bayonets.

Joshua held his broken glasses and ran, half-blind. We proceeded toward a thicket of firs with Salzburg, Valovanchik, and Lerman.

Two hours later, night descended upon the forest. We could finally sit and rest awhile. Joshua hugged me. "You thought I would escape without you, you little *meshugener?*" He kissed me on the head. "I would walk back into Treblinka if it meant I would never be separated from you again." I replied with a lick – the feeling was mutual.

We had no food. The heat of the day had dissipated and it was becoming chilly. Salzburg took a box of matches out of his pocket and started a small campfire. The hoots of owls echoed in low tones, dry leaves crackled under the paws of wolves seeking prey, and flowing sap whispered within the branches.

Lerman pulled down his pants to the light of the flickering flames, and exposed a dirty wound in his hip, the product of a Ukrainian bullet.

"The wound needs to be cleaned," Salzburg said.

"The bullet is still inside," Lerman replied, revealing the severity of his injury.

"If I had a knife, perhaps I could cut it out," Valovanchik said. But no one had a knife.

Lerman pointed at the hem of his shirt and told his friends that he had hidden some money in a secret pocket he'd sewn.

Joshua tried to say something, but Lerman hushed him.

"If you ever do find my Gittel, tell her that her husband died like a man."

His three friends didn't dare look him in the eye. They nodded, staring at the ground.

The flames died down. Joshua and his friends fell asleep. Lerman shivered and moaned. I remained awake, my ears cocked and attentive. Fireflies danced in the dark. As the hours passed, my alertness dulled. Twice I awoke, frightened by the intensity of the slumber that descended upon me. I tried to stand guard, but the hunger and exhaustion got the better of me. I fell asleep, only to be visited once again by the dream.

Not one living creature on Earth.

Mooing cows, baaing goats, mewing cats, and chirping crickets were no more.

I alone remained.

A mark appeared on my flesh.

The brown patch on my chest became a Star of David.

A Jewish ember on four.

A tail-wagging castaway – a lost nomad on the face of the Earth.

A wandering Jewish dog.

I galloped ahead, my ears flapping. I was in a narrow canyon, an endless, winding ravine.

The faces of my ancestors watched me from the rocks.

The clouds of the sky drew together to form the Dog in the Heavens.

The Heavenly Dog barked deeply, an awe-inspiring sight in the skies.

"Do not fear Caleb, my servant. I am your protector, and your reward will be great. Look up at the heavens and number the stars, if indeed you can number them. . . ."

I looked up at the sky as I was commanded.

"No," I replied, "I fear I cannot count them."

"Well," the Heavenly Dog said, sounding slightly disappointed. **"The exact numbering isn't that important. But being that you are a mighty dog, and for the sake of Joshua my servant, fear of the stick and fear of fire are struck from thine heart; I shall place an omen in the sky. I will create a gargantuan dog and make it shine – and its appellation shall be Sirius."**

It was difficult to understand the archaic, biblical dialect of the Heavenly Dog, but that wasn't the end of my troubles. He then asked me to bring him a three-year-old cat. That was beyond my abilities. I had no time to wonder what he meant, as I awoke, terrified, to the sound of a gun cocking. Joshua and his friends started from their sleep as well. We were surrounded by sullen men armed with rifles, fingers on triggers.

We were all terrified – we were trapped! This was it. Our story would end here. This was the way of all flesh. With no trial, in the midst of a thick wood, we'd be shot, and our carcasses left for the birds.

*"Hände hoch, proklyatiye nemzi! Kto dvinetsya poluchit pulyu!"**

"My Russian comrades!" Valovanchik called to them. "I am comrade Valovanchik from Battalion 43, which was defeated in the Battle of the Dnieper. My friends and I were prisoners in the damned Treblinka camp. We revolted and escaped. Embrace us into your troops and we will fight by your side."

A tall, burly man with a thick black beard approached us.

"I am Sasha Molotovski," he said, leaning on his rifle and examining us carefully. "These fine men you see behind me are the vanguard of the East Forest partisan fighters." His eyes lingered upon me. *"Sobaka u vas tozhe yest?"***

Valovanchik nodded. "He belongs to my friend Joshua Gottlieb."

"Can I pet him?"

"Yes, of course," Joshua replied. The large man leaned toward me, ruffling the fur on my head. "I also had a dog," he added sadly.

Then he looked at Lerman. "And what happened to this young man?"

---

* Hands up, you damn Germans. Whoever moves will be shot!
** You have a dog too?

"He was hit by Ukrainian fire," Valovanchik replied, and asked whether they could help.

"We have a doctor," Sasha Molotovski said in his deep voice, and motioned to four of his comrades to lift the wounded Lerman onto a stretcher.

After the stretcher bearers carried him away, Sasha whispered to Joshua, "I don't think your friend has much time left."

Joshua nodded silently.

We followed the partisans into the heart of the forest. We walked for several hours before the pale rays of dawn began seeping into the darkness, accompanied by the chirping of birds.

A sentry stopped us, "Halt! Password!"

Sasha Molotovsky replied, "Victory will come by fist and by gun."

The sentry let us through into the camping area.

A doctor was called to Lerman's stretcher. The doctor, whom everyone treated with much reverence, examined Lerman's injury with grave concern.

In the meantime, our hosts took us to a large table that was set up in the center of the tent camp. Joshua and his friends were invited to sit, and were treated to a loaf of bread and hot tea. I was also treated to a bowl of water and some leftovers. Before their tea had time to cool, Sasha had taught his new fighters their entire doctrine in a nutshell.

"The trees and the dark are your most faithful allies."

"The winter is your friend – its days are short and its nights are long."

"If you're ever surrounded, get out quickly, or you never will."

"Always stay at the enemy's rear, but make him believe that he is chasing you."

"The essence of your strength lies in the element of surprise."

I watched this battle-weary partisan in adoration. He had the fists of a blacksmith, as large as grapefruits.

"Will you give us weapons?" Valovanchik asked.

The bearded partisan laughed. "You want a weapon? There's a rifle on the shoulder of every German soldier!"

CHAPTER 30

A week later, the time had come. The mission: looting food in a nearby village called Drohobych.

Sasha Molotovski laid out the principle: "Partisan fighting is like a ball of mercury that breaks into pieces; it can't be caught, and each fragment reunites effortlessly with the others."

The plan was as follows: we were split into three teams. One would ambush the access road and prevent German reinforcements from arriving, one would enter the village and demand food and clothing for their brother partisans from the farmers, and one – the vanguard – would attack the German patrol.

The team leaders made sure that their weapons were in working order and their knives sharpened, and that the fighters knew their jobs.

At the end of the briefing, Commander Molotovski asked if there were any questions.

Joshua raised his hand. "Can Caleb join us?"

"Of course. Caleb is a partisan like the rest of us."

"Any other questions?"

Silence.

"In that case," he ordered, "everyone must go to sleep now. Wake-up is in five hours. We attack at dawn!"

Before Joshua removed his shoes and lay down on the bed of leaves and rags that he had set up for himself, he reported at the doctor's tent to inquire about Lerman's condition.

"So, tomorrow you're visiting the village and bringing some food?" the doctor asked rhetorically.

Joshua nodded and approached the stretcher that Lerman occupied.

"How is he, doctor?"

"He's sleeping now. I hope tomorrow will be better. This isn't exactly a first-rate hospital, you know."

"Take care of him, doctor. He is a dear friend."

"I'll try," the doctor said. "I promise to try."

There was a scent in the air that I had smelled before. I had smelled it before my eyes even opened, when my weakling brother's head drooped in Kalman's arms. It was a scent that said: open your eyes and cherish this sight, for as you see it today you will not see it again.

We neared the village. A line of twenty partisans. No one spoke. I walked proudly at Joshua's side. Here I was, a fearless partisan pup cutting courageously through the night like a blade. Sleepless birds disturbed the quiet with intermittent chirps, and the insects of the forest clicked and twittered. Dry twigs snapped and crackled under our feet. Twenty pairs of eyes scanned the darkness of the forest for any coming surprises. My snout pulsed with extreme tension. All my scent detectors were vigilant. I identified clear signs of burnt tires. I also picked up the vulnerable scent of newly hatched chicks, the smell of acorns fallen to the ground, wolf droppings, and more. A rich spectrum of odors that couldn't be enumerated. Nonetheless, there was no sign or indication of foe. Several cabins could be seen between the trees at the edge of the forest. A few dogs began to bark. A bored rooster issued his morning call.

The ambush team signaled with a flag that the access road was blocked and that the other teams were free to enter the village. The four houses on the edge of the town were our targets. Three armed partisans entered each house to ensure that the residents wouldn't make a ruckus. The rest of the comrades tied up the cows and goats in the yard.

I advanced with Joshua toward one of the houses. Joshua knocked on the locked door. From inside the house came indiscernible Slavic murmurs.

"Open up!" Joshua called, banging.

Frightened voices could be heard beyond the door.

"Open up!" Joshua called again and kicked the door forcefully. The people inside refused to open. We circled the house and entered from the balcony. A large window covered by wooden blinds was set in the back wall. Joshua struck the blinds. A bolt broke off the rickety wood and the blinds opened with a bang. Joshua and his friends entered through the windows, and I leaped in at their heels. Inside we found an elderly man and woman and their little granddaughter. The aging couple lived in abject poverty.

Their granddaughter was dressed in rags. They begged, but Joshua ignored their cries and grabbed the bags of rice, potatoes, and buckwheat. The terrified child held on tightly to her grandfather's thigh. She started crying. The weeping of young girls always seems loud and contemptible. I barked at her to make her stop, but my barks merely made her wails louder. She hid behind her grandfather and gripped his tattered pajama pants in fear.

"Quiet, Caleb!" Joshua silenced me. "You'll wake the whole village!"

I fell mute.

Joshua approached the old man, who tried to protect his face with his hands.

The old man mumbled something in Polish.

Joshua removed the Pole's glasses and tried them on. They didn't fit, and he returned them to the old man.

We quickly regrouped with the other pillaging teams who had secured their food from the village farmers with punches and cudgels. We headed back toward camp carrying bags of food, jars of fruit preserve, bottles of homemade liquor, eggs, and bread. Naturally, the mood among the partisans was elated. We were followed by two thin cows, three goats, and a pig. Molotovski walked at the head, two chickens held by their feet in each of his hands.

The prevalent estimation was that the supply would last for two weeks. We could eat, we could even be sated, but we had to begin planning the next raid.

We expected to be greeted with cheers, but to our surprise there was much restraint among those who were waiting at the camp. We quickly learned the reason for the gloom. The doctor led us to the bed on which Lerman lay, lifeless, with a bottle of vodka at his side.

"I couldn't prevent his death," the doctor said, "but I tried to take away some of the pain."

I sniffed the body. Despite the long months in Treblinka, I refused to accept the omnipresence of death. That very evening, as Lerman was brought to his final resting place, I paid tribute to his memory with three honorific barks.

Over the next days I experienced a long-lost sensation: satiation. Every evening, the cooks in our group would hide behind the line of pots and pans, and cook up a storm. The forest generously provided onions, mushrooms, and potatoes. Everyone sat around the fire, warming their hands and eating pot roast, chicken soup, and vegetable stew.

I was exceptionally fond of the cows. I admired the peacefulness in which they would lazily chew on grass and leaves. One evening, I followed the cook as he led one of the cows several paces outside of the camp. A tall partisan armed with a knife and a gun accompanied him.

"Have you done this before?" the partisan asked.

"No," the cook replied. "That is, never alone."

"You're supposed to push it on its side first, aren't you?"

The cook tried to hold the cow by its horns and tilt it on its side. The cow struggled and refused to stumble.

"Give me the knife," the cook said, panting. He held the blade at the cow's neck and sliced. The cow bellowed in pain, retreated, and stomped its hind feet. The stream of blood flowed. "Stupid, stubborn animal," the cook muttered angrily.

The partisan couldn't watch the suffering beast. He held his gun to its head and shot.

The cow's eyes glazed over, it pawed the air with a front leg and fell over lifeless.

"It may be stupid, but it knows the difference between life and death."

Molotovski came running, red in the face with anger. He slapped the partisan.

"I've told you a thousand times. You *never* shoot near the camp. Do you want the Germans to come?"

"The cow didn't want to die . . ." the embarrassed partisan mumbled in excuse.

"Enough bullshit!" Molotovski held up a threatening finger. "If you fire outside the camp one more time, I'll shoot *you* in the head. Is that clear?"

The partisan nodded, flustered.

"All right. No more nonsense. I hope you can skin that stupid cow without more gunfire, so I can finally enjoy a nice plate of goulash."

Three hours later, everyone sat around the fire, enjoying the meat and potatoes. As the food disappeared, everyone raised a glass. Molotovski made a toast, the glasses clinked together.

And as they drank, Valovanchik sang:

> "Comrades, let us sing along
> for fear is beaten by a song.
> And to the foe, from the forest night,
> we march, heads high, into the fight!"

The rest joined in for the chorus with enthusiasm:

> "Know, German, that in shadows lie
> the partisans, with watchful eye.
> We'll fill your vile heart with dread,
> with bullets fill your thick, dense head!"

Chicken soup and potatoes weren't the only things cooking in camp. Nearly every evening, a man from the village appeared to relay information. Molotovski paid him generously. The picture was becoming clearer, and the commanders, who used to spend their evenings sitting by the fire singing, now sat planning maneuvers. They would make piles of dirt to convince their friends that their plan was feasible. The commanders would place empty matchboxes between the dirt mounds and call them "Germans." They referred to the carefully placed pebbles as "the ambush," "the attack team," or simply "us." I liked sitting near them and listening to the battle plans. One said they should ambush from the right, and his friend said the left. The first said they should open with a grenade. The second countered that a machine gun would be twice as effective. At times, when they'd reach an impasse, one would turn to me. "Well, Caleb, tell everyone that I'm right." I would reply with a loud bark, and everyone would burst out laughing.

No doubt about it, we Jewish dogs were blessed with a wonderful sense of humor.

CHAPTER 31

A pale mist drowned the trees of the forest. The birds were silent, and even the sound of our footsteps over the fallen leaves was barely heard, thanks to a coat of early morning dew. We had an hour before the dawn broke to reach the road that connected Stryi and Lanivka and conceal ourselves for the ambush. We didn't know exactly what time the supply convoy would pass. We were supposed to wait for Molotovski to signal to us with a flag. Molotovski settled in position at the observation point that overlooked the entire road. Joshua and fourteen other partisans took their place near the point where the road crossed the train tracks. That was where the German supply trucks would be delayed. The first driver, according to our extensive observations, would step out and remove the barrier. That would be the moment for Joshua and his friends to open fire.

The sun had risen, but the fog had not dissipated. The clouds sat heavily above, and light showers came and went.

Joshua rose from our hiding place and headed silently to the observation point. I accompanied him. The path from the ambush to the lookout was arduous. First we had to climb over rocky barricades, then we walked through a muddy wheat field. A creek flowed at the edge of the field, and after crossing it, we had to climb over a tangled, thorny hedge.

"I fear our plan will fail," Joshua said, as he cleaned mud off the bottom of his boots. "The fog is thick and we won't be able to see the signal flag."

"Maybe we have to postpone the mission for a clearer day . . ." Molotovski thought out loud. He sounded hesitant. Joshua's face also revealed that he wasn't happy with that option.

"On the other hand," Molotovski said with more hesitation, "we don't have much food left, and I don't know when the convoy will pass again. . . . Maybe the moment I see the convoy I'll run to join you. . . ."

Joshua shook his head. "It took me fifteen minutes to get here from our ambush location. Besides, if the villagers see you running, they may suspect something."

Molotovski frowned and nodded slowly. A sense of gloom dampened their spirits. It seemed that there was no choice but to reschedule. A large butterfly fluttered between Joshua and Molotovski. I leapt up and tried hopelessly to catch it in my mouth. The failure frustrated me and I barked twice. My barks inspired Joshua, and he said decisively: "We don't need to abort the mission – I have an idea. Caleb will be the sign!"

"Caleb?"

I wanted to ask the same question – Caleb?

"I'll leave him here, tied beside you. The moment you spot the convoy, release him. Caleb will come running to us. The distance that would take us fifteen minutes to cross will take him two. We'll be ready on time."

"Do you trust him? Are you sure he won't suddenly stop to chase a butterfly? Are you sure he'll run straight to you?"

Joshua chuckled, almost scoffing. "I'd bet my life on it."

"You're betting all of our lives!"

Joshua shook Molotovski's hand and said, "I'm not gambling with anyone's life. He'll come running to me. I'm one hundred percent sure."

Joshua returned to the partisans waiting by the barrier.

Molotovski sighed and sat by my side.

"You should have known Sukhoi. I think you two would have gotten along. It was so many years ago, way before you were born. Some dog decided to give birth in our yard. My father, he doesn't play any games. He wouldn't allow dogs in the yard. He took all the puppies and threw them in a barrel of water. They all drowned. All but one. Sukhoi."

I was waiting to hear how the plot unraveled, how Sukhoi finally became a member of their household, but three German supply trucks appeared, raising pillars of dust as they lumbered along the horizon.

CHAPTER 32

I *am Caleb – faster than the wind.* My paws barely touched the ground. I cut through the high stalks like an arrow. I leapt over the thorns like a gazelle and crossed the creek like an otter.

I reached Joshua short of breath. I knew that I mustn't bark. "Good job, Caleb!" He petted my head and addressed his friends. "Wake up! Everyone on the lookout! The trucks will be here any moment."

My belly, which was pressed to the ground, could already feel the rumble of the nearing trucks. My muscles were as taut as violin strings. I looked at Joshua to see if he too felt the moment was imminent.

The trucks slowed down. As expected, the driver of the first truck disembarked to move the barrier. It seemed he intended to call to his friends in the trucks behind his and tell them that the barrier was tied, but he never had the opportunity. Valovanchik's knife sliced through his carotid artery. Valovanchik took the driver's machine gun and removed a magazine with twenty-five bullets from the driver's pocket. He had never used this model of machine gun, but having often watched the Germans in Treblinka use theirs, he more or less figured out how it should be done. He lowered the safety catch, hid near the truck, and signaled to Joshua to throw a grenade. The grenade hit the door of the third truck and fell to the ground without detonating. The truck driver, who must have suspected that something had gone wrong, climbed out of his truck with his weapon drawn. Valovanchik appeared before him and pressed his trigger, but the gun refused to fire. The truck driver leaned his back on the truck, cocked his gun, and started firing in a broad circle toward Valovanchik and the rest of us. The two Germans in the middle truck jumped out with loaded guns. The partisans in the ambush opened fire. One of the Germans fell, injured, before he even shot a single bullet. His friend, terrified, fled.

The driver of the third truck felt around in his pocket, searching for a new magazine. "Charge, Caleb!" Joshua shouted, and slapped my back. He and his friends rose to battle alongside me.

I don't want to give myself more credit than is due, but I swear upon my tail, two fingers from the driver's hand were left in my mouth. He fell on his back and tried to shield his face. The poor man begged for his life, but my ears were deaf to his German pleas. His distinguished Aryan blood stained my whiskers. Then I chased the fleeing driver. The victim's scent of fear inflamed my senses. The driver tried to look back as he ran, lost his balance and fell. I bit his face again and again, like a mad dog. I chewed through him like an eagle picking at a snake.

Within a few minutes, Joshua and his friends joined me. Joshua grabbed my collar and pulled me back.

"Come, Caleb," he said. "Enough! There's nothing more to bite. You've turned him into a meatball!"

We returned to camp heavily laden with goods.

When we arrived, we laid out the plunder. Hundreds of boxes of canned goods, smoked sausages, flour, oil, vinegar, and many kilograms of cabbage. The partisans that had remained in camp under the command of Sergei, the cook, looked at the three newly acquired machine guns and the pile of ammunition that was added to our inventory, and shook their heads in disbelief.

"Quite the raid you guys had," Sergei said with obvious envy.

"Yes," Molotovski admitted, "it was a very successful raid. And we couldn't have done it without this amazing dog!" He leaned toward me and petted me with paternal love.

"Comrades!" he boomed, and everyone fell silent. Joshua listened twice as carefully, because he understood that Molotovski was about to say something about me.

"Comrades! There isn't a dog in the world as smart and brave as our Caleb. I am giving him my medal. From this day on, this dog will be called Comrade Caleb." Everyone laughed. Sergei placed before me a smoked sausage longer than my tail.

"Comrade Caleb is, from today and forever, a partisan with equal rights in our camp. What can I say? When this dog barks, the convoy stops! Oh boy, does it stop!"

CHAPTER 33

O ur blessed partisan routine didn't last long. The *Stuka* air sorties over the forest became more and more frequent, and many German soldiers flowed to our neck of the woods. Our raids in the villages became more dangerous and less common. Joshua's health wasn't great either. His coughing at night became worse, and at times he would shiver for hours under our ragged blanket.

One night I tossed and turned. It had been weeks since we had carried out a successful foray, and our food supply was becoming scant. Enemy aircraft hovered over us from dusk to dawn and we were forced to spend long hours under camouflage nets. The hunger was bothersome and Joshua's loud coughs made it difficult to sleep. And then, in the dead of night, the camp sentry sounded the alarm whistle. The slumbering partisans awoke as one to their greatest nightmare. That which we feared was upon us. German troops were raiding the forest, making their way with the deadly fire of machine guns. Mortar shells were falling from the sky.

"Burn everything and run!" Molotovski cried, but no one heard his orders. Everyone had dispersed every which way. Some partisans tried to return fire, but there was no chance. The Germans had absolute superiority in personnel and in arms. My comrades were dropping like flies before my eyes. A long, terrifying burst of shots hit the tree I was hiding behind. I ran, panicked, wherever my legs would carry me. I looked all around, searching for Joshua to no avail. I was fear-stricken. Bullets flew over my head. I knew all about human tools of destruction and the death they wrought.

A sudden stabbing pain paralyzed my thigh, and I fell, wounded. I was hit. The smell of blood flooded my senses. My blood. I turned my head to lick the wound, but blood streamed all over my fur. Every movement brought another wave of unbearable pain. It was clear – the injury was severe. I lay down, ready to let go. My war was ending. The battle didn't interest me anymore. The explosions were dull in my ears. My last thoughts were of Joshua. Was he still alive? My looming death did not trouble me. Short and bitter were the days of my life!

My thoughts blurred. Suddenly, the sky was darkened by cumulus clouds. Torrential rain poured down unabated from the heavens. Buckets of water fell fiercely. The ground became muddy. The German uniforms soaked through. German commands of retreat echoed between the trees.

"Caleb . . . Caleb. . . ." I heard a voice calling me. Was it the voice of the Heavenly Dog?

"Caleb . . . Caleb. . . ." The voice became more human. "Caleb!" I now recognized it as Joshua's worried, desperate voice.

I opened my eyes. Joshua was standing above me.

"Caleb, you're alive!" He hugged me. "You're alive! You're alive!"

Three partisans came and stood at his side.

"He's severely injured," one of the partisans said. "He's in pain."

"I'll put him out of his misery," another said, reaching for his gun.

"No!" Joshua cried, and shielded me with his arms. "If you shoot him, you kill us both."

"I had a dog once," the partisan said. "My entire childhood, I grew up with dogs."

Joshua hesitated.

"The poor thing is suffering," the partisan with the rifle tried to convince him. "We mustn't delay. The Germans might come back at any moment. We have to run!"

"I'm staying."

"Jew, don't be stupid. How will you survive alone in the forest for even one day?"

"God will help."

"Like He's helping now?" mocked the man holding the rifle.

Joshua didn't reply.

Joshua sat with me in the blood-soaked forest until the first light. The cold air threatened to freeze us to death. My bullet-ridden comrades lay lifeless, their faces sunken in the muddy ground. A terrible lament was carried silently in the wind. Angels were crying for the forest heroes who had fallen by sword. At night I was haunted by my dreams, and I kept waking. Each time I fell asleep, I worried I'd never wake up again.

The Heavenly Dog came to me again and tried to encourage me. **"Do not fear Caleb, my servant. I am your shield, and your reward will be great. Look up at the heavens and number the stars, if indeed you can number them. . . ."**

The pain was unbearable. All I could see was stars.

When the sun peeked from the horizon, flies swarmed toward my wound. I didn't have the strength to banish them. Joshua swatted at the flies, but they came back quickly. He picked me up and carried me to the nearest village.

"Caleb, my heart and soul," he whispered in my ear, and I could hear the strain in his voice. "I don't know if I'm bringing you to recovery or to your grave."

Although he feared that the villagers might hand us over to our enemies, he gathered his courage and walked toward the houses. The villagers were uneducated, impoverished, and teeming with superstition. Turning in a Jew was, to them, like squashing a bug. It was obvious we'd need a miracle.

CHAPTER 34

*A*nd a miracle we were granted. The miracle was named Olga Berdyczewski. A nicely-rounded woman, her bosom filled her peasant dress to the brim. To quote Joshua, "an entire orchard should be planted in her honor."

I don't know if it was her fondness for dogs, her fondness for Jews, or both that caused her to take us into her home.

"My dog has been injured," Joshua said, and she quickly improvised an operating table for me.

"I need sausages, and vodka too," Joshua requested. "Lots of vodka."

Soon Joshua presented me with a dozen sausages doused in a scent that made my head spin.

He petted my head. "If you don't wake up . . ." he said, his voice quivering. "If you don't wake up. . . ."

I couldn't hear the end of his sentence. When I bit into my third sausage, my senses grew numb and my sight dimmed. Despite the pain, I understood more or less what Joshua intended to do. I vividly remembered how I was drugged by the men in black coats, back when I spent the night with Margo on a newspaper in the underbelly of the city. I had seen how a doctor cut into the belly of a partisan who had been given a bottle that smelled just like my sausages. And yet, I put my destiny in Joshua's hands without hesitation.

I couldn't eat the last sausages. My head became heavy and my tongue fell limp outside my mouth. Beyond the screen of intoxication, I could feel myself being tied to the table. Olga shaved the fur off my thigh with scissors and a razor, and Joshua cut into my skin with a white-hot knife. It was the only pain I ever felt that I would not wish on my most bitter enemies. Joshua cut something out of my body and stitched the open wound with a thread.

For the first days after the surgery, I couldn't eat or drink. Olga made chicken soup, and Joshua soaked an old shirt in it, and then squeezed it into my mouth. It was a month before I was ready to get up from my bed and walk on all fours.

Joshua was hidden away in dark corners. I, on the other hand, was allowed to run around Olga's house and yard. At first I preferred to stay in Joshua's company, but I quickly got tired of hiding, and began wandering around the house.

I especially liked sitting by Olga's goose pen. She had five geese, and a couple chickens as well.

Olga hid Joshua in a small space underneath the barn floor. She covered the space with a wooden plank, and covered that with a pile of hay. In the morning, warm rays of sun would shine through the big barn window straight onto the haystack. At that time of day, I would climb onto the haystack, circle myself several times, making a comfortable little spot, and leave my thigh exposed to the healing caress of the sun. Twice a day, Olga would bring a bottle of water and a pot of baked potatoes for Joshua. Sometimes she would vary the menu and bring zucchini and eggs.

I would sit under the table and watch Olga as she cooked. Her thick arms jiggled as she peeled potatoes and crumbled bread to feed her geese.

Olga would wake up early in the morning. First she would heat a pot of water to wash herself and a pot of milk for her morning meal. Then she would feed the poultry and collect their eggs. Every day she would dust off the display case in the living room. Many books were arranged on the shelves, but I never saw her open one.

One day, as she was dusting, loud knocks were heard at the door.

"Gestapo!" a voice called from beyond the door. "Open up!"

Four Gestapo officers entered the house and scanned it quickly.

"Where is the landlord?"

"I am the landlord. I'm widowed."

From where I sat on the haystack, I could hear the moving of furniture. The officers came into the yard and approached the barn.

"And what's under the haystack?"

"There's nothing under there," Olga lied. "It's just the poor dog that lies here. Officer, I don't know if you've ever adopted a dog, but this dog is really quite sick. I found him injured, losing lots of blood, infested with fleas, with thick saliva coming out of his mouth. I'm not sure it's a good idea to go near him."

I rose from my curled up position and twitched my head. I lifted one leg, and sank back down with my tongue out. The officers watched me with pitying looks. I stood up again and limped toward them, wagging my tail weakly, my tongue hanging. I swear upon my tail, they believed every move, and disappeared before I could lick one of their hands.

Once, toward evening, Olga came to the hiding place carrying a pot of potatoes and carrots. "Five months ago, they killed my husband," she told Joshua. "Jezhi was the youngest of the Drohovski family, the richest family in the village. People would come from Vienna to buy their horses. Five thousand zloty per horse!"

She removed the cover from the pot. "Eat, eat," she urged Joshua. "And give some to the dog. Just because you're nice enough to listen to my stories doesn't mean you have to starve while you do it."

Joshua stuck a fork into one of the potatoes and bit in.

"All the village girls wanted to marry my Jezhi. He wasn't like the other men in the village. He was educated. He taught math and literature at the Gymnasium. But Jezhi didn't want anyone else, only me. He told me that I was a 'round figure' – it was his kind of joke. When the Germans came, they turned the Gymnasium into a command center. Instead of young boys playing in the yard, there were armored vehicles. A German soldier stopped Jezhi when he was on his way home from the tavern. My poor, drunk Jezhi." Tears welled in her eyes. "He greeted the soldier with curses and spat in his face. And the soldier shot him again and again without stopping, riddling his body with holes. My poor Jezhi, he never had a chance."

Joshua held out his hand and they embraced for a long time.

"May God save your kind soul," Joshua whispered to her. "I fear that you will pay with your life for the mercy that you have shown me."

She tightened her grip on his hand. "Better to be killed by German fire than to roast in the fires of hell."

One afternoon, a blond boy sneaked into the barnyard. He lay down on the haystack, in my usual place, and listened carefully. An evil streak flashed in his blue eyes. A rumor had spread that several Jews were hiding around the village. Ignorant, hate-filled young boys were hungry for a hunt. I knew that if I tried to bark out a warning, I would merely raise suspicion. But what could I do? Was I doomed to watch Joshua taken out of his hiding place and led to his death?

The boy ran off. I knew he'd be back.

A few minutes before sunrise, as I was asleep in Joshua's arms, we heard noises coming from the barn. Someone was lifting the haystack that covered our hiding place. I heard shouts coming from outside. Joshua held me close, and I could hear his rapid heartbeat.

The wooden planks that served as our ceiling were wrenched away, and a happy, round face looked at us from above. It was Olga's shining smile. She seemed even plumper and happier than usual.

"Come on up," she called to us, clapping her hands. "It's over! The war has ended!"

Joshua exited the hiding place and blinked. He hadn't seen sunlight in months. The sun slowly rose and lit the earth with an optimistic, pale light. There was no sweeter sound than this announcement, the end of the war.

Olga and Joshua sat together on a tree stump in the yard and watched the green hills and the meager flocks grazing. It was the time for survivors. The vista seemed delicate and brushed, a pleasant backdrop for the memories carried by the wind of those who died by fire and those who died by water.

"Stay with me," Olga asked. "I will be a good friend, a loyal wife."

"Olga my dear, my savior. You are a beautiful woman, and your heart is bigger than the world itself. But I am a Jew and I cannot marry you."

"What's the difference between the God of the slaughtered and the God of the butchers?" Olga asked. "I don't care for either. And I certainly can't understand why you still follow the God that let the Germans lead your brothers into the furnaces and did nothing about it."

Joshua took her hand gently and kissed her cheek.

She awaited his answer, but he was in no rush to reply. A peaceful quiet lingered between them, and the attentive listener could hear the chirping of birds alongside the ding-dong of cattle bells.

"Just as a dog follows his master, I must follow mine. The dog of a righteous man follows him, as the dog of an evil man follows *him*. I don't know if my God is righteous or evil, but He is my master, and I am willing to die for His name."

"But He watched your parents, your brothers, and your

friends get butchered, and didn't lift a finger!"

Joshua said nothing and looked toward the horizon. They continued holding hands and let the hours pass.

"I need someone to help me with the lumber before winter and with the potatoes in the spring. Look what I have left. A handful of geese and chickens. You know what I had before the war? Five milking goats, and I can't even count how many chickens and geese. The partisans took them all. Even worse than the Germans! The Germans put a bullet in your head and – pop! – that's it. The partisans starve you bit by bit.

"I'll stay with you for a while. But I can't stay longer on this land soaked in the blood of my brothers. Europe has cast us out. Caleb and I have no choice but to sail to the land of Israel."

Olga stroked my head and smiled at me lovingly.

"I'll miss the little *pisher*."

Joshua added a stroke of his own and answered for me. "I'm sure the little *pisher* will miss you too."

"And when you reach the Land of Israel, will you send me money?"

"What's mine is yours. I swear by everything holy that I won't rest until I send you enough money to buy seven fat, beautiful goats."

Joshua had made his decision. Worn out and sickly, his skin shriveled and his hair thinning, he had nothing left in Europe and would sail to the blossoming Jewish garden, the Land of Israel.

CHAPTER 35

"Certificate!" demanded the Jew in the grey coat, standing on the pier next to the ship *Tekumah*, holding the rope barrier in his hand. Joshua presented his papers. The Jew flipped through the paperwork with a blank expression. First he made sure that no documents were missing. Then he double-checked the validity of the certificates and the validity of the signatures.

He looked carefully at Joshua's face and compared it to the face in the picture.

"How old are you?" he asked.

"Twenty-five."

The man examined Joshua with suspicion.

"What I've seen and what I've been through has aged me prematurely. I am not very healthy," explained Joshua, and coughed twice to make his point. His coughs were sharp and hollow.

"Here you go," the man said, and returned the certificates to their owner. He lowered the rope. "You can go through, sir, but the dog must stay here. Direct orders from the ship commander, sir. Absolutely no animals on board."

Bloody Cossack, I thought, and watched Joshua, waiting for what he would say.

"The dog comes with me!" Pride and might were apparent in his eyes and voice. "This dog shared a bed with me in Treblinka for months. He refused food so I could eat. This dog stood by me as I watched the smoke pillars rising from the crematoria, carrying my brothers and sisters away. This dog fought beside me with the partisans, and he hid with me in a musty cellar for many, many months. This dog is no less Jewish than you or I. Our nation is his, and our God is his. Where I go, he goes. Either we both board, or we both stay."

The man softened. "Wait here," he requested. "I'll speak with the captain."

A few minutes later, he returned. "Choose a room at the very bottom, deep in the belly of the ship. And don't let his snout out the door. If anyone sees him, they'll throw you both into the sea."

One night, Joshua decided to disobey the captain. He took me with him to the upper deck. We watched the dark waters together. "Do you see, Caleb?" he said. "Do you see this huge sea? On the ground there are wars, and man seeks to control every bit of land, but the sea remains immune. The water stirs quietly and sends foam to the beach, and the fish swim in the depths like they have since creation. Look carefully at the sea, Caleb my dear. A day will come when this sea will unite us."

I didn't quite follow his point, but it was clear that he had told me a great secret. He kissed me on the forehead and we returned to our room in the ship's hold.

At some point during our voyage, we met a Jew named Elijah. Elijah was a tall man with a tangled beard and a patch over his right eye. After a few minutes of conversation, Joshua and Elijah shook hands. They discovered that Elijah knew Joshua's family.

"And what about the rest of the family? Is there anyone left?"

Joshua said nothing.

"It's just you?"

"Yes," he mumbled. "It's just the two of us."

Elijah said that Adolf Hitler, may his name be blotted out, had a dog too. The dog's name was Blondi. When the tyrant understood that his game was up, he poisoned his dog and then killed himself, along with his beloved, Eva Braun.

Every dog has his day, I thought.

Joshua petted my head and said, "The living dog is better than the dead lion."

Hark, nations of the world! He who poisons Jews will ultimately end up poisoning himself, his wife, and his beloved dog!

CHAPTER 36

*I*n the Land of Israel, we settled near the beach in a small village called Tel Aviv. Although bones didn't grow on trees and *gefilte* fish didn't swim in the Yarkon River, Israel was a wonderful place. Men and women walked the streets without fear, and spoke Yiddish spiced with the language of Abraham. Every now and then, through the open window, I heard men calling in Yiddish, "*Alte zachen, alte zachen.* . . ."* Their accent didn't remind me of any specific *shtetl.***

We settled in a small building, two stories tall, that housed three tenants. Above us on the top floor lived Martin Hoffenbach, a God-fearing violinist whose face fondly reminded me of Kalman Gottlieb. I liked lying on his doormat and listening to him play.

The apartment on the ground floor was occupied solely by Mrs. Simchayoff, a heavy woman with gold rings and bracelets, a gold watch, gold teeth, and a heart of gold. The

---

* Old things, old things. . . .
** village

previous winter she had taken in a tiny, black kitten who was blind in both eyes. I couldn't believe that out of all the cats in town, she chose the blind one. *Catz in a zack,** I thought to myself. I couldn't ignore its resemblance to the cat Karl Gustav had killed in the park. Mrs. Simchayoff told Joshua that the kitten's life had been in great danger, as the infection in his eyes almost left him paralyzed. The kitten had spent a week under medical supervision, clinging to life by his tiny claws, but now he was feeling much better.

I was fond of the cat, who was named Parshandatha, and I treated him with respect and mercy. It was amusing to watch him find his way between the furniture in the Simchayoff household, or try to catch a fly with the help of his triangular radar-like ears.

All Mrs. Simchayoff had to do was move one of the pieces of furniture, and little Parshandatha would be completely lost. It took him a long time to adjust to the new arrangement. The little half-wit, *catzisher moyech,*** would even have trouble finding his food dish. He would walk into a wall, and his soft face showed simple astonishment. I once heard Joshua suggest jokingly to Mrs. Simchayoff that she put Braille signs on the wall.

When I saw the kitten struggling in his search for the food dish, I shook my head in amusement, *wer is de catz und wer is dir putar.**** I let him hold on to the edge of my tail and I'd lead him to the bowl that Mrs. Simchayoff set

---

* a cat in a sack

** cat-brain

*** Literally: where is the cat and where is the butter. Meaning: if you find the butter, the cat must be nearby.

up for him. I gladly acted as his guide dog. Joshua told me that Mrs. Simchayoff had a place in heaven saved right next Olga Berdyczewski, on the dais of honor. The Master of the Universe repaid those who saved the helpless.

Joshua acclimated nicely and established friendly, neighborly relationships with all the families – old and new – that lived nearby. On Friday nights, we could hear Shabbat songs floating in from the neighboring houses, and at the end of the meal, Joshua's friends would visit us and bring me a sizeable portion of leftovers. Jews from all over the globe came to enrich my bowl with the splendors of their kitchens. I was lucky enough to taste kibbeh, kababs, moussaka, chorba, chulent, couscous, goulash, and stuffed artichokes. For the first time in my life, I had to raise my paws in defeat and say, "Enough, thank you, I'm full." Fresh schnitzel placed in my dish would try to entice me to take a bite, but I defiantly declared, "No! There's no more room in my belly!"

The years of famine were over.

After Friday night dinners, I would doze in the yard and get the holy dirt of Israel all over my fur. I felt wonderfully Zionistic. My mouth absorbed immigration and my stomach united Diasporas. Joshua would come and sit by my side. He would open the Book of Books and read me the adventures of Joshua and Caleb – the biblical *Palmach**

---

* The elite fighting force of the Haganah, the underground army of the Jewish community during the period of the British Mandate.

warriors – who, just like us, had a long, difficult journey on their way to the Land of Israel.

On weekdays, weather permitting, we would go on a morning walk along the beach. I would run on the sand and Joshua would look into the horizon and silently ponder. Once we met an old man, short and bald, who seemed to have large cotton wads glued above his ears. Joshua waved at him and whispered to me that this man was the alpha male of the Israeli pack.

The days, weeks, and months passed pleasantly. Joshua and I barely parted, and therein, of course, lay the secret of happiness. Unlike the cold European years, the years in Tel Aviv were mostly summer and very little winter. The summer sets a lazy tone, tempting you to go to the beach. What could be better than playing in the sand, licking up salt water, and *schnorring* pieces of meat from the generous barbeque chefs who chose the beach as the prime location for their art? I made two good friends at the time. Azit, a fearless female with suicidal tendencies, and Balak, a slightly unstable and fickle Jerusalemite.

I was no longer a young dog, and Joshua's health was also poor. Nonetheless, we lived every day to the fullest, appreciating these years of calm. And indeed, everything was peaceful, until that strange evening, two years after we settled in Israel.

There was an odd tension in the air that evening, as though everyone was waiting for a heaping serving of pleasure. It was similar to my feeling each time Mrs. Simchayoff began removing steaks from her grill. All the residents sat glued to their radios and listened carefully. They held pencils and, with shaking hands, filled out a three-columned table. At the end of the radio ceremony, everyone came streaming out of their houses, waving flags, singing and dancing in the city squares. Joshua was too ill to dance in the streets. The weakness from his war wounds hadn't yet left his body. He sat on the balcony, watching the celebrating crowd with sheer happiness in his eyes.

That night, before we went to sleep, Joshua said the *Shema* prayer. As he said "Love the Lord your God . . ." he began to cry bitterly.

He spoke to the darkness.

"Why did You look away when my parents and siblings were gassed to death? Why did You stay silent when Your children were burned to dust?"

I had questions of my own. "Why do You let neglected dogs die, exhausted? Why don't You help blind cats who are starving to death?"

Joshua went on. "Why would You command me to love You, and then do everything to make me hate You?"

I licked the tears that flowed like water. These tears were the last drink that I tasted.

"And though You did everything You could do to make me hate You . . ." he stopped himself from crying, "I still love You. I never stumbled in this commandment. He read the verse again. "Love the Lord your God with all your heart, with all your soul, and with all your might."

I knew that this time God was listening from the heavens.

"My God and the God of my forefathers," Joshua said. "I've seen enough! Caleb is old and sick. His legs are failing him. The gleam has left his fur and his teeth are falling out. And I am not exactly healthy anymore either. I'm sick of missing them! All I ask is this: Take us both to Hershel and Reizel. Please, don't separate us again. The separation is a wound that will never heal, the blood will never clot. Take us together to Father and Mother."

His prayer was answered.

That night, we went to sleep and never awoke.

Loved and admired in their lives, and in their death not parted.

EPILOGUE

For a moment in the dead of the night, the skies of Tel Aviv were flooded by a pure light, and our souls mounted a lightweight cherub and flew through eighteen thousand worlds. Suns and comets lit our way, and puppy-planets greeted us with cheerful barks.

"Here they come! Here they come!" one of the junior angels called.

The angels aligned in two rows along the cloud-carpet that led to the throne. Ministering angels stood with their chins up, looking straight into eternity. A mustached angel ordered *"Wings hut!"* and everyone raised their wings in salute. We walked along the cloud-carpet together, reviewing the sleek formation.

We stood before the throne.

The Heavenly Dog lay curled up at the feet of the Master of the Universe.

The Master of the Universe shook Joshua's hand warmly and joked around a little in Yiddish.

The Heavenly Dog and I sniffed each other in restraint and wagged our tails.

The Master of the Universe instructed one of His helpers to accompany Joshua to the white escalator to Paradise.

"And what about Caleb?" Joshua asked.

"Caleb?!" replied the Master of the Universe.

"The dog."

"Ah, yes, yes. Of course. We have a special paradise for Jewish dogs, with endless grassy knolls and dog food like manna."

"No, Sir!" Joshua said, and the Master of the Universe raised a puzzled eyebrow.

It seemed He was not accustomed to hearing "No."

"Pardon my rudeness, just this once."

The Master of the Universe leaned back on his throne, and repeated, "No?!"

Gabriel and Michael, who stood on either side of Him, looked angry and drew their swords.

The Master of the Universe chided them.

The swords were returned to their sheaths.

"No, Sir!" Joshua said again, with as much uncompromising forcefulness as he had addressed the gatekeeper of the *Tekumah* ship. "I raised Caleb from the day he was born. You separated us once, and I swore on Your name that we would not be separated again. Caleb licked my skin after it was branded with a number. Caleb was the only spark that led me in the dark. We were in hell together – and together we will march into Paradise. There is no force in the world that can tear us apart. Not even You."

The Master of the Universe said nothing.

"This is the deal," Joshua said, like a real Jew who knows how to bargain with God. "I won't start any scandals, won't ask any questions like 'How could You?' or 'Where were

You?' 'Why did You hide Your grace?' and 'Why did You stay silent?' – and You let me stay with Caleb. Well? What do You say?"

"It's not so simple," Gabriel intervened. "Do not forget that the ways of the Lord are mysterious."

Look at him, I thought, the Almighty's defense attorney.

Joshua looked straight at the Master of the Universe, waiting for His answer.

The Master of the Universe looked to His right and to His left, gauging Michael and Gabriel's reactions. They both nodded their heads, indicating that the deal seemed quite fair and sensible to them.

"*Nu, shoin,*"* God said. "It's late, and I don't feel like arguing."

I wanted to approach Him and thank Him with a lick, but Joshua pulled me back and whispered that it wasn't appropriate. Before we turned toward the escalator, the Master of the Universe asked that we wait for just one moment.

"Come here, Caleb," He said.

I approached Him, and He petted my head fondly.

"Do you remember what the Heavenly Dog said? 'Your reward will be great!'"

"I remember," I barked.

"Well, I have a little surprise for you. . . ."

The Master of the Universe snapped His fingers and Ezekiel came running.

"Do you have the portion we saved for Caleb?"

"Of course," Ezekiel replied. He rushed off and returned

---

* Well, all right

two minutes later pushing a wheelbarrow filled with dry bones.

And Caleb saw Joshua mount the white escalator and, dragging the wheelbarrow behind him, he ascended.